Auschwitz Lullaby

Auschwitz
Lullaby

MARIO ESCOBAR

THOMAS NELSON
Since 1798

Auschwitz Lullaby

Published in Nashville, Tennessee, by Thomas Nelson. Thomas Nelson is a registered trademark of HarperCollins Christian Publishing, Inc.

Translated by Gretchen Abernathy.

The English translation for the lullaby at the end of chapter 1: Good evening, good night, covered with roses and carnations all round, slip under the covers. / Tomorrow morning, if God wills, you will wake once again. / Tomorrow morning, if God wills, you will wake once again. / Good evening, good night, watched by angels who show you in your dreams the Christ-child's tree. / Sleep now blissfully and sweetly, see paradise in your dreams. / Sleep now blissfully and sweetly, see paradise in your dreams.

The epigraphs are from (1) Elie Wiesel, Romanian-born Jewish writer, survivor of Nazi concentration camps (in *US News & World Report*, October 27, 1986; quoted in Christian Volz, *Six Ethics: A Rights-Based Approach to Establishing an Objective Common Morality* [eBookIt.com, 2014], ebook, section "Essay 3: Social Justice"); (2) Miklós Nyiszli, Hungarian Jewish doctor; assistant to Dr. Mengele (in *Fui asistente del Doctor Mengele: Recuerdos de un médico internado en Auschwitz* [Osweicim: Frap-Books, 2011]; quotation in translation); and (3) Olga Lengyel, Hungarian doctor and Auschwitz survivor (in *Five Chimneys: A Woman Survivor's True Story of Auschwitz* [Chicago: Ziff-Davis, 1947], 212).

Thomas Nelson titles may be purchased in bulk for educational, business, fund-raising, or sales promotional use. For information, please e-mail SpecialMarkets@ThomasNelson.com.

ISBN: 978-0-7852-1995-8 (trade paper)

Library of Congress Cataloging-in-Publication Data
CIP data is available upon request.

Printed in the United States of America
18 19 20 21 LSC 5 4 3 2 1

*To my beloved wife, Elisabeth, who visited
Auschwitz with me and fell in love with this story.
I want to spend the rest of my life with you.*

—

*To the more than twenty thousand ethnic Gypsies
who were imprisoned and exterminated in Auschwitz
and to the quarter million murdered in the forests
and ditches of northern Europe and Russia.*

—

*To the Asociación de la Memoria del Genocidio
Gitano (Association for Remembering the Gypsy
Genocide), for their fight for truth and justice.*

The opposite of love is not hate, it's indifference. The opposite of beauty is not ugliness, it's indifference. The opposite of faith is not heresy, it's indifference. And the opposite of life is not death, but indifference between life and death.

—ELIE WIESEL

An hour after leaving Kraków our convoy stopped at a large station. The sign gave the name of the place: Auschwitz. That doesn't mean anything to us. We'd never heard of the place.

—MIKLÓS NYISZLI

One required an extraordinary moral force to teeter on the brink of the Nazi infamy and not plunge into the pit. Yet I saw many internees cling to their human dignity to the very end. The Nazis succeeded in degrading them physically, but they could not debase them morally.

—OLGA LENGYEL

AUTHOR'S NOTE

Auschwitz Lullaby has been the hardest book of my entire professional career to write—but not because of any formal difficulties with the writing or quandaries about where the story was headed. What worried me was not being able to capture the greatness of Helene Hannemann's soul within the lines of these pages.

Human beings are momentary breaths in the midst of the hurricane of our circumstances, but the story of Helene reminds us that we can be the masters of our own destiny, even though the entire world is literally against us. I cannot say if this book has taught me to be a better person, but certainly to offer fewer excuses for my errors and weaknesses.

When Larry Downs, my friend and publisher, heard Helene's story, he said the world needed to know it. But that does not depend on us . . . It's up to you, dear reader, and your love for truth and justice. Help me to tell the world the story of Helene Hannemann and her five children.

> Madrid, March 7, 2015
> (just over seventy years after
> the liberation of Auschwitz)

PROLOGUE

MARCH 1956
BUENOS AIRES

I held my breath during the airplane's steep ascent. I'd hardly even stepped outside the capital city the entire six years I've spent in Argentina. The thought of being cooped up in such a small space for so many hours made my chest hurt, but as the plane's nose evened out, so did my breathing, and I calmed down.

When the attractive blonde came up and asked if I wanted anything to drink, I told her tea would be fine. For a second I thought about having something stronger, for my nerves, but since my stay in Auschwitz, I had snubbed alcoholic beverages. It was a disgrace to see my colleagues drunk day in and day out, and Commandant Rudolf Höss barely batting an eye. It was true that in those final months of the war, desperation had overtaken many men. Some had lost their wives and children in the barbaric Allied air raids. Still, a German soldier—and even more so a member of the SS—should remain collected regardless of the circumstances.

The stewardess carefully placed my hot tea on the tray table, and I flashed her a smile. She had perfect features. Her lips were just wide enough, her eyes a bright, intense blue, her cheeks small and rosy—the ideal Aryan face. Then I turned my eyes to my old black leather case. I had packed a couple of biology and genetics texts to make the trip go faster. I cannot explain why, but at the last minute I also decided to grab a couple of the old notebooks from the *Zigeunerlager* kindergarten in Auschwitz-Birkenau. Years before I had put them with my reports on genetic studies carried out in Auschwitz, but I had never gone back to read through them. The notebooks were the diaries of a German woman I met in Auschwitz, Helene Hannemann. Frau Hannemann and her family, and the war, were now part of a distant past I preferred not to dwell in, the years when I was a young SS officer and everyone knew me as Herr Doktor Mengele.

I reached over and picked up the first notebook. The cover was completely faded, the corners were stained with dried splotches, and the paper had taken on that faded yellow color of old stories no one cares about anymore. Swallowing my first sip of tea, I slowly opened to the first page. The long, slanting hand of Helene Hannemann, the director of the Gypsy nursery school at Auschwitz, took me back to Birkenau, to section BIIe, where the Roma were housed. Mud, electric fences, and the sweet smell of death—that was Auschwitz for us, what it remained in our memories.

ONE

MAY 1943
BERLIN

It was still dark when I stumbled half-asleep out of bed. Though it was starting to get warm during the day, the mornings continued to be chilly enough to give me goose bumps. I slipped into my light satin robe and, without waking Johann, headed for the bathroom. Fortunately, our apartment still had hot water, and I could take a quick shower before going to wake the children. All of them but little Adalia had school that morning. I wiped the steam off the mirror with my hand and looked at myself for a few seconds, noting how the encroaching wrinkles seemed to make my blue eyes look smaller. I had bags under my eyes, but that was not surprising for a mother with five children under the age of twelve and who worked double shifts

1

nursing to keep the family afloat. I toweled off my hair 'til it recovered its straw-blonde color, but I stopped to examine the gray streaks that were spreading upward from my temples. I got to work curling my hair, but that only lasted until I heard the twins, Emily and Ernest, calling me. I threw my clothes on and, still barefoot, hurried to the other bedroom.

They were sitting up in bed chatting quietly when I entered the room. Their two older brothers remained curled up, grasping at the last few seconds of sleep. Adalia still slept with us, as the kids' bed was too small for all five of them to squeeze in.

"Less noise, sweeties. The others are still sleeping. I have to get breakfast ready," I whispered. They beamed at me as if the simple sight of my face were enough to make their day.

I pulled their clothes off the chair and placed them on the bed. The twins were already six years old and did not need my help getting dressed. The more people there are in a family, the more streamlined the systems have to be to help everyone get the simple tasks done as quickly and easily as possible.

I went into our tiny kitchen and started heating things up. A few minutes later, the bitter scent of cheap coffee filled the room. That weak substitute of brown-tinted water was the only way to cover the tastelessness of our watered-down milk, though by now the older kids knew they were not drinking real milk. Every now and then with a bit of luck, we could get our hands on a few cans of powdered milk, but since the beginning of the year, rations had grown even scarcer as things got worse on the front.

The children came racing to the kitchen, elbowing their way through the narrow hallway. They knew the bit of bread with butter and sugar that they were offered every morning would not linger long on the table.

"Less noise, please, loves. Your father and Adalia are still in bed," I scolded as they took their seats. Despite their hunger, they did not tear into the bread until I had handed around the mugs and we had prayed a short prayer of thanks for our food.

Three seconds later the bread had disappeared and the children were downing their coffee before heading to the bathroom to brush their teeth. I took that moment to go to our room, get my shoes and coat, and put on my nurse's hat. I knew that Johann was awake, but he always played possum until he heard the front door close. He was ashamed that I was the family's breadwinner now, but everything had changed in Germany since the war began.

Johann was a violin virtuoso. He had played for years in the Berlin Philharmonic, but since 1936, the restrictions against everyone who did not fit into the Nazi Party's racial laws had grown much harsher. My husband was Romani, though most Germans used words like *Gypsy* or *tzigane* to describe people of his race. In April and May of 1940, practically his entire family had been deported to Poland. We had not heard anything from them in nearly three years. Fortunately, in the Nazis' eyes I was a purebred; because of that, they had not bothered us since then. Even so, every time someone knocked on our door or the phone rang at night, my heart jumped involuntarily.

When I got to the front door, the four older children were waiting with their coats buttoned, their school caps on, and their brown leather satchels at their feet. I looked them over, tied on their scarves, and dawdled at the part of the routine when I kissed their cheeks. Blaz, the oldest, sometimes pushed my effusive affection away, but Otis and the twins ate up those precious moments before we crossed the threshold to walk to school.

"Come on, I don't want you to be late. I've only got twenty minutes 'til my shift starts," I said, opening the door.

We had hardly made it onto the landing and flipped on the light when we heard the clop of boots noisily ascending the wooden stairs. A chill ran up my spine. I swallowed hard and tried to smile at the children, who had turned to look at me, sensing my unease. I gave a nonchalant wave of the hand to reassure them, and we started to go down. The children dared not leave my side. Typically I had to keep them from dashing headlong down the stairs, but the approaching footsteps quelled their energy. They crept along behind me, as if my lightweight green jacket might conceal and protect them.

By the time we got to the second-floor landing, the sound of the boots filled up the entire stairwell. Blaz leaned over the rail to get a look and one second later turned back to give me the look that only an older brother can give to communicate what he knows without upsetting the younger ones.

My heart starting racing then. I could not breathe, but I kept going down the stairs hoping that once again misfortune would simply pass me by. I did not want to believe that suffering had chosen me that time.

The policemen ran into us right in the middle of the second flight of stairs. The agents were young, dressed in dark-green uniforms with leather belts and gold buttons. They stopped directly in front of us. For a silent moment my children looked in awe at their pointed helmets with the golden eagle, but then they dropped their eyes to the level of their shiny boots. A sergeant stepped forward, panting a bit, looked us over, and then began to speak. His long Prussian-style mustache shook with his politely threatening words.

"Frau Hannemann, I'm afraid you'll need to return to your apartment with us."

I looked straight into his eyes before answering. The cold reply of his green pupils pierced me with fear, but I tried to remain calm and smile.

"Sergeant, I'm afraid I don't understand what's going on. I need to take my children to school and then get to work. Is anything the matter?"

"Frau Hannemann, I would prefer that we speak in your apartment," he answered, forcefully taking my arm.

His movement startled the children, though he had intended to be subtle. For years we had witnessed the violence and aggression of the Nazis, but this was the first time I felt actually threatened personally. I had hoped for so long they would simply fail to notice us. The best way to survive in the new Germany was to be invisible.

The door of some neighbors, the Wegeners, opened ever so slightly, and through the crack I glimpsed a pale, wrinkle-creased face. She gave me an anguished look, then opened the door all the way.

"Herr *Polizei*, my neighbor Frau Hannemann is a wonderful wife and mother. She and her family are the model of politeness and goodness. I hope no ill-intentioned person has defamed them," Frau Wegener said.

That act of bravery brought tears to my eyes. No one

risked public exposure in front of the authorities in the middle of the war. I looked into my neighbor's cataract-clouded eyes and squeezed her shoulder gratefully.

"We are only following orders. We simply want to speak with your neighbor. Please, go inside and let us do our job in peace," the sergeant said, grabbing the doorknob and slamming the door shut.

The children jumped, and Emily began to cry. I seized the moment to pick her up and press her against my chest. The only words that managed to cut through the grief and solidify in my brain were, "I won't let anyone hurt you, children."

A few seconds later, we were standing in front of our apartment. I fished for the key in my purse stuffed with crackers, tissues, papers, and makeup, but one of the policemen pushed me aside and rapped hard on the door with his fist.

The sound echoed down the stairs. It was still quite early, and the city had not yet emerged from the silence of the night. People were just beginning their morning routines, trying to hide in a normalcy that had ceased to exist a long time ago.

We heard hurried steps, and then the door opened, casting light onto the landing. Johann's mess of dark, curly hair partly covered his eyes, giving him a distinctly disheveled appearance. He looked first at the police, then at us. Our eyes silently pleaded with him to somehow protect us, but all he could do was push the door open all the way and let us in.

"Johann Hanstein?" the sergeant asked.

"Yes, Herr *Polizei*," my husband answered with a trembling voice.

"By order of the *Reichsführer-SS* Heinrich Himmler, all Sinti and Roma of the Reich must be interned in special camps," the sergeant recited. Surely he had repeated this speech dozens of times in recent days.

"But . . . ," my husband started. His big black eyes seemed to devour the eternal instant before the policeman made a sign and his colleagues surrounded my husband and held his arms.

I placed my hand on the sergeant's shoulder. "No, please. You'll terrify the children."

I could sense a slight heaviness in his gaze for a few seconds. Ideas never manage to completely suffocate feeling. A German woman who might be his sister or cousin was talking to him, not a dangerous criminal intent on deceiving him.

"Please allow my husband to get dressed. I'll take the children into another room," I pleaded with him softly, trying to alleviate the violent situation.

The sergeant waved his men away from Johann. But then he barked, "The children are also coming with us."

Those words were the knife that shredded my insides. I doubled over in the throes of nausea, shaking my head to clear what I had certainly misheard. Where did they want to take my family?

"The children are also Romani. The order includes them as well. Don't worry, you yourself can stay," the sergeant said, trying to explain the new situation to me. Surely my face finally registered the desperation that I had been feeling for many years now.

I tried to argue. "But their mother is German."

"That makes no difference. There's one child missing. My information says there are five children and one father." The sergeant's tone was serious.

I could not respond. Fear had paralyzed me. I tried to swallow back my tears. The children had their eyes glued on me the whole time.

"I'll get them ready in a moment. We'll all go with you. The youngest one is still in bed." I was surprised to hear my voice. The words seemed to come out of some other woman's lips.

"You will not come, Frau Hannemann, only those with tzigane blood, Gypsies," the sergeant said dryly.

"Herr *Polizei*, I will go where my family goes. Please let me pack our bags and get my youngest daughter dressed."

The policeman frowned but waved me out of the room

with the children. We went to the main bedroom, and, climbing on a chair, I took down the two large cardboard suitcases we kept on top of the wardrobe. I put them on the bed and started putting clothes inside. The children surrounded me in silence. They did not cry, though their anxious faces could not conceal their concern.

"Where are we going, Mama?" asked Blaz, the oldest.

"They're taking us to something like a summer camp, like I showed you once when you were little. Do you remember?" I said, forcing a smile.

"We're going to camp?" Otis, the next oldest, asked. His voice had risen with confused excitement.

"Yes, sweetie. We'll spend some time there. Remember I told you a few years ago your cousins were taken away too? Maybe we'll even see them," I said, attempting an upbeat tone.

The twins really did get excited then, as if my words made them forget everything they had just seen.

"Can we bring the ball? And some skates and other toys?" Ernest asked. He was always ready to organize a plan for playing.

"We'll only take what we absolutely need. I'm sure there are plenty of things for children where we're going." I desperately wanted to believe it might be true.

I knew the Nazis had dragged Jews away from their

homes, as well as political dissidents and traitors. We had heard rumors that the Reich's "enemies" were interned at concentration camps, but we posed no threat to the Nazis. Surely they would just require us to stay within the bounds of some sort of improvised camp until the war ended.

Adalia woke up then and got scared when she saw the mess on the bed. I picked her up. She was a skinny little three-year-old, with soft features and very pale skin. She was very different from her older siblings, who looked more like their father.

"It's okay, nothing's wrong, honey. We're going on a trip," I said, holding her tight against my chest.

I felt a heavy lump in my throat, and the flood of worry washed over me again. I thought that I should call my parents, that they should at least know where we were being taken, but I doubted the police would let me make a call.

After getting Adalia dressed, I finished with the suitcases and went to the kitchen. I packed a few tins, the little bit of milk we had left, some bread, the remaining scraps of cold cuts, and some crackers. I had no idea how long our journey would take, and I wanted to be prepared.

Back in our tiny living room, I realized my husband was still in his pajamas. I put the two heavy suitcases down and went back to the room to find him some clothes. I picked out his best suit, a brown tie, a hat, and a coat. While he changed under the steely watch of the police, I returned to our room and took off my nurse's uniform. The children were lined up against the door, not letting me out of their sight. I picked out a suit with a brown jacket and blue blouse and got dressed the best I could with the younger three all crowded around me. We went back to the living room, and I studied Johann for a moment. Dressed so elegantly, he looked like a Gypsy prince. He put his hat on when I entered the room, and the three policemen turned toward me.

"There's no need for you to come, Frau Hannemann," the sergeant insisted.

I looked straight into his eyes and asked, "Do you think a mother would leave her children in a situation like this?"

"You'd be shocked if I told you all I've seen in the past few years," he answered. "Very well, come with us to the station. We have to get them to the train before ten o'clock."

His comment made me think the trip would be longer than what I had first thought. My husband's family had been deported somewhere to the north, but I presumed they would be taking us to the Gypsy internment camp they had built near Berlin.

We went through the living room to the doorway. My

husband went first with the suitcases, the two younger policemen on his heels. Then my two older sons, the twins clinging to my coat, and Adalia in my arms. When we stepped out the door onto the landing, I turned to look one last time at our home. I had woken up that morning with the unthinking confidence that we had a normal day ahead of us. Blaz had been a bit nervous about a test he had before recess; Otis had complained of a bad earache, a sure sign he was about to get sick; the twins were healthy as horses but had still grumbled about having to get up so early for school; Adalia was a little angel who always behaved well and tried her best to keep up with her siblings in their games. There had been no sign, no omen that all of this normalcy would amount to nothing a short time later.

The stairwell was not well lit, but a faint glow of early morning sun reached us from the entryway below. For a second I had the stabbing pain of leaving my home, but no, that was not quite right; my home was my five children and Johann. I closed our apartment door and began to descend the stairs, humming the lullaby my children always requested when they were upset or had trouble sleeping. The unspoken words flooded the hollow of the stairwell and calmed the children's hearts as we headed into the unknown.

MARIO ESCOBAR

Guten Abend, gute Nacht,
mit Rosen bedacht,
mit Näglein besteckt,
schlupf unter die Deck:
Morgen früh, wenn Gott will,
wirst du wieder geweckt,
morgen früh, wenn Gott will,
wirst du wieder geweckt.
Guten Abend, gute Nacht,
von Englein bewacht,
die zeigen im Traum
dir Christkindleins Baum:
Schlaf nur selig und süß,
schau im Traum's Paradies,
schlaf nur selig und süß,
schau im Traum's Paradies.

TWO

MAY 1943
ROAD TO AUSCHWITZ

Everything happened really fast. In the loading and unloading zone of the train station, hundreds of people were crammed onto the platforms. At first we were rather dazed. The police had left us with a group of SS soldiers, who in turn had pushed us inside the station. I was startled to see a dark-brown cattle car with its doors wide open, but it did not take me long to understand what was going on. I was still holding Adalia, but now with the other hand I grabbed the cold but sweaty hands of the twins. The older two were clinging to the suitcases Johann was gripping as tightly as he could. The soldiers started pushing us, and the platform slowly emptied as people struggled to get into the cattle cars. Johann set the suitcases down and helped Blaz and Otis get in. Then he lifted the twins into the car.

Just then, the pressure from the crowd started to drive me forward. Johann had gotten into the car so I could hand Adalia up to him, but it was all I could do to stay within arm's reach of the car door. Johann grabbed Adalia, but I found myself farther and farther away. A human sea of men, women, and children was sweeping me toward other cars. With my heart heaving, I tried to fight my way back. I took hold of a metal bar on the car and jumped hard, suspended for a split second above the heads of the passing crowd, but a crack at my ribs caught me up short. I turned and saw an SS soldier trying to pry me away with his nightstick. My husband could see what was happening. He crept along the opening of the car to where I was holding my free arm out to him. Our eyes locked as a second blow almost knocked me back down into the crowd. I managed to reach Johann's hand, and he pulled me into the car.

I barely controlled the impulse to vomit as the nauseating stench of the car hit me. It was bad in there. We managed to carve out a space for the children to sit on the hay that reeked of urine and mold. Johann and I stood. With nearly a hundred people crammed inside the car, few could sit.

The train lurched forward and started to advance

slowly. The movement threw us off balance, but the huddle of bodies all around kept us from falling. The hellish journey had only begun.

Everyone in the train was Gypsy like my husband. At first, people tried to remain calm. But as the hours passed, arguments and fights broke out. Four or five hours in, thirst became a serious issue. Babies were screaming inconsolably, children were hungry, and the elderly were starting to faint from exhaustion and the uncomfortable positions we all were forced to maintain. The train car never stopped lurching and clattering. Despite the fact that it was the beginning of May, it was cold. German afternoons are very cold, and we were headed away from the sun.

By nightfall, panic was setting in until one of the older Gypsy men raised his voice above the din in his ancestral tongue. That managed to calm people down a bit. Johann and a few of the men helped organize the car and mark off one of the corners as a sort of latrine, with a bucket and a blanket hanging down from the ceiling to provide a modicum of privacy.

I seized the moment to give my children a bit of food and a few sips of milk one at a time. The two older ones threw themselves back down on the hay, the twins curled up in the hollows at their feet, and Adalia slipped into the middle.

There was no light, but none was needed to imagine the fear and sadness on all the travelers' faces. The conditions in which we were transported allowed us no illusions about the kind of life we were being taken to. When Johann returned from setting up the latrine, I could not hold back any longer. I broke down on his shoulder. I tried to muffle my sobs in his jacket so the children would not wake. But tears brought no relief. The harder I cried, the more desperate I felt.

"Don't cry, sweetie. Things will surely get better when we get to the camp. In '36 a lot of Gypsies were interned for the sake of the Olympics, but a few months later they were allowed to return home." Johann's tone was soothing. It was the first time we had spoken since that morning. I allowed myself to be relaxed by the timbre of his voice, as if nothing bad could happen if I stayed by his side.

"I love you," I said, hugging him. How many times since we first met had I told him how I felt. But to love him in that place, surrounded by a desperate horde, was the confirmation of all those years of uninterrupted fidelity.

"The Roma have been persecuted for centuries, and we've always survived. We'll find a way out of this," Johann said, stroking my face.

We had been together over twenty years. We met when we were young and his family showed up in Freital, the town outside of Dresden where I was born. My parents were active in our church's outreach projects and helped the Gypsy children integrate into the community. As soon as they saw Johann, they knew he was special. My parents had to overcome the prejudices that have always existed against the Gypsies. Most of our neighbors thought Gypsies could never be trusted. At any moment they might be lying or trying to cheat you. My father got to be friends with Johann's father. His family was mainly in the business of buying and selling horses, but they also sold all sorts of things. Sometimes Johann's dad would come to our house to show us the latest things he had gotten ahold of: table linens hand-sewn in Portugal, sheets, fine towels . . . My mother distrustfully scrutinized the fabric but almost always ended up giving her approval. The two men would wrangle a few moments over the price and then seal the deal with a handshake.

Meanwhile, my eyes were for the boy. With his pronounced cheekbones and square chin, he was every bit the Persian prince to me. Yet we hardly ever spoke. Sometimes we were allowed to play ball in the yard, but we would only look at each other and kick the ball back and forth. My parents took a liking to him. They got him into our elementary school and made sure he made it through high school; then they paid out of their own pocket for him to study at the conservatory.

One morning Johann's father brought an old pocket watch by our house and swore to my father that it was quartz with gold inlay. After haggling for a while, my father bought the watch. Within two weeks, it had stopped working, and the gold had turned to brass. The two men did not speak for quite some time, but my parents continued supporting Johann. Little by little, as we would walk together to the conservatory, my feelings for him started to grow. Johann did not propose until he had finished his degree. And it did not take him long to become one of the country's finest violinists.

When I told my parents I was in love with Johann, they warned me to think it over well before making a wrong move. We came from very different cultures. In the end, love overcame the obstacles and prejudices of the world around us. Naturally, we suffered a great deal after we married. The laws against Gypsies were very strict. And Gypsies did not like mixing their blood with non-Gypsies, even though they were a bit more lenient in the case of men. Johann had to swear to my parents that he would not be an itinerant Roma. When his family left our town, he came to live at our house.

I remember the days leading up to the wedding. The entire town seemed to be on edge. One of the pastors from our church came to try to dissuade us from contracting what he considered an "unnatural union," but even so, we were happy and went on with our plans. The morning we went to the office to register the marriage and request the civil ceremony, the office staff refused to give us the certificate. Only the intervention of a kind-faced, elderly judge restored the due process of law.

Now all those memories and hardships seemed a million miles away, a mere drop in the bucket of the deep, terrifying abyss we were rattling into.

The next morning we stopped for a few hours in Pruszków, which confirmed that we were in Poland. Thirst was starting to drive us mad. The stench of vomit, urine, and feces was everywhere, the air nearly unbreathable. Then we heard a rumor that an SS soldier was peering through the car's one tiny window. People were begging him for water and food.

Pointing his Luger through the window, he shouted, "Give me everything of value you've got!"

Johann helped the other passengers gather up wristwatches, rings, and other jewelry so the soldier would give us fresh water. One pail, that was all. It was precious little for nearly one hundred people, barely a sip for each. People were panting and desperate, losing the manners they had tried so hard to maintain. When it was our turn, Adalia drank first, just a few tiny sips, then the twins and then Otis.

Blaz looked at me, his lips dried. He handed me the pail without drinking. He understood there were sick people and babies who needed it more than he did. It brought tears to my eyes. His courage stunned me: he would deal with his own thirst so that others could satisfy theirs.

By the afternoon of that second day, several children in the car had high fevers, and some of the older passengers seemed truly ill. We had now gone a day and a half with almost no food or water and hardly any sleep.

The second night was even worse than the first. An old man named Roth had a heart attack and sank down right next to us. There was nothing we could do for him. The children were terrified, but we managed to get them to sleep.

"How much longer will we be here?" I asked Johann, my head resting on his shoulder.

"I don't think it will be much longer. The camp's got to be in Poland. With the way the war is going, they must still have camps open there for prisoners," Johann said.

I hoped he was right. As a nurse, I knew that the children would start dying after two or three days without food or water, then the elderly and the weaker adults. We only had one more day to hold out in these appalling conditions.

Our dire straits made me recall our first home. We moved into the house of Johann's aunt and uncle on the outskirts of town. They let us sleep in a small, dank room, but the mere fact of being together made us happy enough that we spent most nights laughing under the sheets, trying not to bother the older adults. One time when I was home without Johann, his aunt started in on me, accusing me of thinking I was a big shot and of doing nothing to help around the house. She berated me with insults, then kicked me out. It was snowing like crazy outside. I sat on top of our suitcases, soaked and shivering and waiting for Johann to get home.

As soon as he saw me, he hugged me and tried to pass me all his body heat. We spent that night in a hostel and the next day found a small house to rent with a kitchen and a tiny bathroom. Two weeks later, Johann got the position at the conservatory, and things started looking up. We no longer had to survive on canned food and fight to stretch our marks to the end of the month.

The third day of our cattle-car journey began especially cold. We stopped once again, and the same soldier from the day before offered us a bit of water in exchange for more jewelry and valuable objects. The water calmed us down momentarily, but thirst reared up even more fiercely after the tempting dribble. Five people fainted on the journey, though the saddest part was when a baby died in the arms of his young Gypsy mother, Alice. Her family members begged her to put the child in the area where we had piled the other cadavers, but she clung to the lifeless body of her baby. I knew that within hours I would be in her shoes. My heart broke at the thought. I remembered all the nights of waiting up with my children, all the happy days we had spent together. I could not make sense of it. My children were completely innocent. Their one crime was having a Gypsy father. This war was driving the whole world crazy.

Night fell once again. Beside me, the children lay totally still. The poor things had no strength left. Exhaustion, thirst, and hunger had all but snuffed out their lives, like candles about to be extinguished. Johann held Adalia in his arms. She was wan and her skin so dry from dehydration. All she wanted to do was sleep.

I picked my way to the wooden slats of the car's wall to see what I could see through the cracks. I could make out a huge station with a central tower. People stirred more and more the longer we were stopped there. Then we were moving again, passing under an arch of some sort. On the other side, a long barbed-wire fence secured to concrete posts stretched out along the railway. Powerful floodlights lit up the camp. It looked huge and horrible, but at least it was somewhere to live, a way to escape the infernal train.

People grew restless when we stopped again, but four hours passed without anyone coming up to the train. Exhausted, we all slouched and curled up the best we could, a tangled mess trying hard to avoid the cadavers and to get some sleep. The mother of the dead baby was the only one who stayed close to the dead bodies, as if already resigned to being swept away by the shadows.

My family slept fitfully, dancing at the edge of death, and I began to weep in silence. I felt guilty for not having foreseen that the Nazi lunacy would end up getting us in the end. We should have fled to Spain or to America, tried to get as far away as possible from the madness that had possessed our country and nearly all of Europe. I had always wanted to believe that people would wake up and see what Hitler and his followers represented, but no one did. Everyone went right along with his fanatical insanity and turned the world into a starving, warring hell.

When daylight finally came, we heard the barking of dogs and the stomping of feet over the gravel around the railroad. Fifty soldiers, an SS official, and an interpreter who repeated the orders in several languages woke everyone in the train.

We were all eager to get out of the train's nightmarish conditions, unaware that we were jumping from the frying pan into the fire.

"Quiet now," I said to the children. They looked at me placidly. They were very tired, though they were also curious about what waited for us outside.

As the train car began to empty, Johann picked up our suitcases, and we looked all around before jumping down. A huge multitude was descending from the train cars. Below, SS soldiers and prisoners dressed in striped uniforms were separating everyone into different lines.

"Get out quickly!" one of the soldiers shouted at us.

Johann jumped down and then helped the rest of us. My legs were wobbly, and my bones ached, the cold of the place slicing to the deepest parts of me. The SS soldiers had dogs and were carrying nightsticks in their hands, but it did not seem like they were going to use them. A few yards away there were watchtowers and in the background huge smokestacks, but we hardly had time to look at what was right around us.

They divided us into two huge groups: women and children on one side, men on the other. At first I tried to resist being separated from Johann, clutching his hand until one of the prisoners came up and softly said, "You'll see him later. Don't worry, ma'am."

Johann handed me the suitcases and stepped into the other line. We held each other's gaze. He tried to smile to reassure us, but his lips contorted into unbearable anguish, not mirth.

"Where are they taking Daddy?" Emily asked as she rubbed her red eyes.

AUSCHWITZ LULLABY

I did not know how to answer. I was speechless, made completely mute from grief. My brain simply could not process the meaninglessness of it all. I just stroked her head and lowered my eyes so she would not see my tears.

"Men between twenty and forty years of age will come with us," one of the SS officials said.

The group split into two, and I watched Johann being taken away from us. He was at the front of the line, so I only had a few brief seconds to watch his wide back and dark, curly hair partly tucked into the neck of his shirt. My existence had revolved around my husband for many years now. My soul emptied as he walked away. Life was not worth living without him. Then I looked at our children. They studied me with their wide eyes, trying to read my heart. Then I understood that being a mother is much more than raising children; it is bending the soul until the self is forever mixed up in their beautiful, innocent faces. The group of men was now a good distance away, and I was still biting my lips to keep from crying. Johann was walking deep inside the formation, his face hidden from me. I begged heaven to let me see him one more time. Soldiers were pushing and hurrying the men, but Johann took the momentary risk. He turned and caught me with his eyes, those beautiful pupils more than making up for words.

27

THREE

MAY 1943
AUSCHWITZ

As our line advanced alongside the interminable barbed-wire fence, my fears took on phantasmagorical shapes. Interrupted only by short embankments of grass, an endless succession of wooden barracks stretched before us, like shipwrecked vessels along an infinite coast. All around them, like disoriented castaways, people dressed in rags stared at us indifferently. I thought it must be some sort of mental hospital. Shaved heads, striped uniforms, absent expressions on the faces first of the women we passed, and then of the men—surely they were signs of dementia. Who were all these people? Why had they brought us here?

An eerily sweet smell permeated the place, and gray smoke clouded the first timid rays of the morning sun.

Meanwhile, the female guards drove us at a martial speed and never stopped giving orders. We walked for quite a while until we came to a movable fence. They made us go through. The children were worn out and hungry, but they did not let us stop to give them anything to eat. They made us stand for nearly two hours in front of a small building of rough wood with a German sign that said "Registration."

Finally, a strikingly beautiful guard, dressed in an official dark-green uniform and cape, began shouting at us to enter the building. There, four women in prisoner's dress who looked a bit better than the ones we had seen at the edge of the camp handed us a green sheet of paper where we were to write down our names and personal information, along with a white sheet of paper from the Reich Central Office that ordered our immediate internment at the camp. It took me some time to finish the paperwork for my five children. Adalia would not let me put her down, and the rest were clinging to my coat.

"Faster, woman. We don't have all day," a female prisoner worker told me impatiently.

There was a long line behind me. We moved forward to the second table, where some men were tattooing onto the new arrivals' bodies the number we had been assigned on the green paper. I held out my arm and the pricks hurt, but the prisoner finished quickly.

With no expression in his voice, he said, "The children too."

"The children?" I said, horrified.

"Yes, those are the orders." The man's eyes were blank behind his round glasses. He seemed more like a robot than a human, completely devoid of feeling.

Blaz, the oldest, stretched out his arm without hesitating, and once again my mother's heart broke with pride in him. Right away, Otis followed suit and then the twins. They bawled a bit at the pain, but none of them pulled away or refused the tattoo.

"The little girl's arm is so thin," I said, indicating Adalia.

"We'll do her thigh," the prisoner answered.

I had to pull Adalia's white tights down and reveal her milky white leg for the man to mar it with the number preceded by Z for *Zigeuner*, Gypsy.

We left the building and got back into the long line, this time waiting for the female guards to escort us to the Gypsy camp. We stood there for at least an hour while a fine spring rain soaked us to the bone. The children were so exhausted and hungry they hardly moved.

The pretty guard—later I learned her name was Irma Grese—ordered us to start walking. We followed her in a long line along the edge of a small forest that was starting to turn green after the harsh Polish winter. The contrast between the trees full of life and the muddy streets of the camp made me think about the miserable human condition: only we were capable of destroying natural beauty and turning the world into an inhospitable place.

We came to a huge gate and continued on to a wide street that marked the entry to the Gypsy camp the Germans called "Zigeunerlager Auschwitz." On each side there were long barracks that served as kitchens and storehouses, followed by some thirty more barracks for prisoner residences, a hospital, and bathrooms.

The paper they had given us apparently had the number of the barrack where we were supposed to reside, but we were all so overwhelmed, exhausted, and hungry that we followed like zombies, unaware of where we were going or what we were doing.

The guards grew impatient. With the help of some prisoners, they grabbed the papers from our hands and pushed us toward our assigned barracks. Finally, I pulled myself together, and before one of the prisoners wielding something like a nightstick could hit me, I figured out we had been assigned to barrack number 4.

The main road was nothing but mud, and when we got to our supposed new home, we were surprised to see huge mud puddles inside as well. Water was pouring through the roof and dripping through the wooden walls made of bent, poorly secured planks. The barrack was literally a foul stable where not even animals would have deigned to sleep. That is what we were to the Nazis, wild animals, and that is how they treated us.

Our new pigsty home reeked of sweat, urine, and filth. A large brick oven about four feet high divided the room in two. On each side there were three rows of beds the prisoners called *koias*. There were up to twenty people crammed into each of these wooden cages. People were supposed to sleep on bare wood, and the only protection was a shredded blanket, typically flea-ridden. Precious few had sacks stuffed with sawdust to resemble a straw mattress. But there were not enough of these "beds" for everyone, and some prisoners had to sleep on the muddy ground or on the stone bench that ran the length of the barrack.

"Is there a free space anywhere?" I asked some women sitting on the bench. They looked me over and started to cackle. None of them spoke our language. They had to be Russian Gypsies.

With our suitcases still in my hands, I searched for somewhere to go, but there was no room anywhere. The children started to whimper. They had been standing almost all day long with nothing to eat.

One of the women, the block scribe—that is what they called those who did the daily prisoner count—told us there was a bit of space in the last row of *koias* at the back, but that my oldest son and I would have to sleep on the floor until more space opened up.

I did not understand. How could space just open up? Did that mean some people got to go home? At that thought, the faint hope fluttered through my heart that I might see Johann again and return to our normal life. Maybe when the war was over, everything would go back to normal. Unfortunately, I later realized that she was talking about prisoners dying, whether because of the inhumane living conditions or because the guards outright killed them.

The children tried to crawl up into the *koia*, but the block supervisor told us there were prescribed hours for rest and the guards forbade use of the beds until nightfall.

I took a deep breath and put the suitcases down where my children would sleep that night. Blaz asked if he could go out, and though it was still raining, I thought it would be better for him to breathe clean air instead of the putrid, depressing air of the barrack.

"Where are the bathrooms and the showers?" I asked the scribe.

"In the last barracks at the end of the camp, numbers 35 and 36, but you can only go in the morning and at a set time in the afternoon. The showers are only for the morning." She frowned at me, seemingly bothered by my many questions. Her strong Russian accent slurred the words, and it was hard for me to understand.

"But what about the children?" I asked.

"They have to go in the corner of the barrack, and the adults hold it until we're allowed to go. At night there's a bucket, and new arrivals like you have to empty it when it gets full."

My insides churned just thinking about it. I could just imagine how the urine would reach the brim of the bucket in a few hours and I would have to go out to the embankment to empty it in the freezing dark.

"Everyone has to be inside the barracks within half an hour. Then they'll bring supper and after that we can't go out until tomorrow morning. If you're caught outside the barracks, the punishment is severe," the scribe said in a matter-of-fact tone.

I could not understand anything. The rules seemed absurd and arbitrary. I had been working in hospitals for years as a nurse, and I knew that order was necessary for things to function, but the logic I was hearing was irrational.

I took the children to the bathroom. Blaz was nearby talking with a group of boys, but when he saw us, he left them and followed us.

"What is this place, Mom?" he asked.

I knew I could not fool him. The other kids had gotten

distracted playing in a puddle, so I squatted down and tried to help him understand the situation. "We're being held here for being Gypsies," I explained. "I don't know how long we'll have to stay, but we should try to lie low, go unnoticed. We've only been here a few hours, but I think it's best we avoid drawing attention to ourselves."

"Okay, I'll try. I'll take care of the little ones and try to find us some food."

"Let's go get cleaned up a bit," I answered, ruffling his dark hair.

When we entered the bathroom barrack, my heart sank. It smelled even worse than the sleeping barracks. There was something like an animal feeding trough that was utterly foul, and at the back a long concrete slab with holes that served as one long, continuous toilet. We went up to the trough. The water was dark brown and smelled like sulfur. I could not believe my eyes. How was I supposed to wash the children in that? It was a veritable petri dish of infection.

"Don't touch the water!" I shrieked as Otis moved to take a drink.

"But we're thirsty," he whined.

"That water is infected," I said, drawing them away from the long sink.

Their eyes grew large in disbelief. Their faces black with the dirt of long days in the cattle car, their dehydrated skin, the dark circles under their eyes, and their bodies limp from hunger—it all rendered me speechless. I wanted to wake up from that nightmare, but I could not give in. That is what I thought about as I tried to hold back my rage. For the first time in my life I did not know what to do or say.

We returned to the barrack right at the end of what they called the free hour. Everyone was returning to the barracks, and within minutes the wide central avenue was completely deserted.

We headed back to the place we had been assigned, and I bent forward to take the pajamas out of our suitcases. I was surprised to find them open. When I pushed back the cover, I saw there was barely a scrap of clothing left. The little bit of food we had brought, my coat, and the rest of our belongings had disappeared. I could not take it anymore, and I started to weep. Now all we had left was what we were wearing and whatever food they would bring us that night.

I heard laughter behind me, which enraged me. One of the women was hiding one of my children's shirts under her blanket. With two long strides I reached her *koia* and jerked back the blanket.

"What are you doing, German frau?" she screamed with a heavy accent.

"That's ours," I answered, grabbing the shirt and pulling.

Another woman yanked my hair bun, and when I tried

to push her hands away, the first woman slapped me in the face. One of the barrack guards, a fellow prisoner, came up to us. These women were responsible for maintaining order inside the barracks, like the prisoner overseers, the *kapos*, were to do outside.

"Quiet!" she said, yanking me backward.

"They stole from me!"

"That's not true," one of the women answered. "This cursed Nazi is just stirring up trouble."

"Is that so?" the guard asked.

"No! They took everything we had," I answered with palpable rage.

"It's your word against theirs. Get back to your bed and don't cause problems. Otherwise we'll let the *Blockführer* know, and you'll be punished. You're a mother. You'd better stay out of trouble with other internees," the guard said, pushing me back to our bed.

I returned to our *koia* with my face bruised and feeling utterly powerless, but I knew the prisoner guard was right. Ten minutes later, two prisoners entered with a large container that held a disproportionately meager amount of a stale black bread whose principal ingredients were sawdust, a spoonful of margarine, and a bit of beet compote. This was supposed to nourish us until the next day. The prisoners and the children quickly lined up with little bowls. A woman handed me a bowl with the rations for my five children and me. I was almost the last to receive the food. When the children saw what I had brought them to eat, they hesitated for a moment, but hunger took over, and they gobbled it down in seconds. I preferred to give them my portion. I knew that it would only carry them a little while longer, but perhaps it would be enough until the next morning.

It quickly grew difficult to see. There was no electricity in the barracks, and when night fell, we all had to go to bed and try to sleep. Outside, it had stopped raining, but the water still seeped in through the walls and around the floor. I took Adalia's boots off her and put Blaz on boot duty. Then I helped the twins lie down beside her. There were four other women in the *koia* with them who jostled them until their backs were pinned against the wet wood of the barrack wall. Then Otis got in, slipping between the women and his siblings and managing to secure a bit more space for them all, much to the protests of the uncomfortable bedfellows. There was hardly any light left in the barrack, just enough to look momentarily at the faces of my four youngest children. They seemed to be at peace despite the horror that surrounded us. I swore that I would do the impossible for them to survive. Then I stretched the blanket over them and turned to Blaz, who had climbed onto the rock bench with the other blanket.

"Mom, come get some rest. I'm sure we'll see things in a better light tomorrow," he said with a smile.

We snuggled together, trying to keep our balance and not fall into the mud. Blaz fell asleep almost instantly. I listened to his slow, measured breaths and then noticed the final whimpers and complaints of the other prisoners with their children. We were in a rancid stable surrounded by strangers. My husband, Johann, had disappeared, and the future was so uncertain that the only thing I had strength to do was say a weak prayer for my family. I had not been to church in nearly seven years, but at that moment, speaking into the inexorable vacuum of that hangar seemed like the only way to grasp at a shred of hope. My thoughts were jumbled and confused. Hunger, fear, and anguish drowned my mind, as if living in that camp were like trying to breathe underwater. I thought again of my husband's beautiful face. His eyes said it all. I would see him again. He would not leave me alone, not even in hell. Johann, like Orpheus who passed through the underworld to save his wife, would come to rescue me from the clutches of death itself; though that night I thought of how I would suffer the same fate as Eurydice, and my beloved would remain on the other side of the Styx. The night lasted forever. I hardly slept, broken by fear and uncertainty but determined not to give in. My children would be my strength until Johann came back for us.

FOUR

MAY 1943
AUSCHWITZ

Our arrival at Auschwitz could not have gone worse. I still had not understood that the only rule that governed the camp was to survive at any cost and not expect help from anyone. Mothers snatched up the tiniest morsels of bread to feed their emaciated children; men came to blows over better camp jobs with the hope of surviving one more day. The female guards and the SS took advantage of our vulnerable situation in the cruelest and most sadistic ways. The logic of Auschwitz could not be compared with what reigned on the other side of the electric barbed-wire fences.

They woke us when there were still two hours left before dawn. We had to rush to get dressed, tidy up the barrack, and take advantage of the few minutes we were allowed to go to the bathroom. It was not easy to get my five children ready with such little time, but Blaz helped with Adalia while I tended to the others. Our shoes splashed in the mud as we ran to the bathrooms. We had to wait outside in the rain until it was our turn. I sent the children in first to do their business, but we had taken in such little liquid and food that nothing came out. Then I decided to wash their faces and hands with the freezing water in the troughs that served as sinks.

"Don't drink even a drop of this water," I warned them. You did not have to be a nurse to recognize that that water was far from drinkable.

We had hardly managed to wipe ourselves off when the kapos pushed us out to make room for the next people.

When we went back out to the main road, our hands and faces still wet, the cold of the Polish morning sliced through us. I did not even want to think about what it would be like in autumn or winter, when the thermometers rarely registered anything over freezing temperatures.

As we returned to the barrack, I tried to pay more attention to the camp buildings and surroundings. All the barracks looked the same on the outside except the ones closest to the bathrooms. One was called "Sauna," which was for disinfecting the prisoners, and another one stood nearby, but I could not tell what it was for. Barracks 24 to 30 seemed to be hospital pavilions for men and women. It comforted me slightly to think that the camp was concerned for our health, and I thought I might offer to volunteer there. Perhaps that would even improve our position in the camp. The remaining barracks were all for sleeping, though the ones at the front of the camp were also offices and sleeping quarters for the kapos, with more amenities than what the rest of the prisoners had.

They made us stand in line for a very long hour until the morning count to make sure no one was missing. Then we went back inside our barrack and got out the one bowl we had been given the night before. Two of the kitchen workers served a dark, foul-smelling liquid they called coffee. I went up to one and asked, "Is there any milk for the children?"

The woman stared at me, turned to her coworker, and snarled, "The duchess wants some milk for her little princes." Turning back to me, she said, "I hate to tell you, but blue blood doesn't get rank in here."

The rest of the women in the barrack cackled hoarsely at me, so I took the coffee and went back to my children without saying a word.

They took small sips of the drink. At least it was something warm to take the edge off the morning cold and fool our stomachs for a bit. We still had another half hour free.

I preferred to go back outside instead of staying cooped up in that foul place. We made our way toward the barracks at the entryway. We saw the offices, the kitchens, and the storerooms. Most of the people we saw working turned out to be common criminals, as I later learned, though some were Gypsies. I moved to speak to one of the women in the office, but no sooner had I taken a step than one of the guards blocked my way.

"Where do you think you're going?" she said, raising her whip.

"I wanted to ask a question," I answered, meeting her gaze. The children instinctively drew closer to me.

"This is no summer camp. Does your housing assignment not quite meet your expectations? Do you have a suggestion for the cook? Get back to your barrack, you slut," she said as her fist cracked into my cheekbone.

Blood gushed out of my nose and soaked my clothes. The children cried with fear, but Blaz stepped forward to defend me.

"No, Blaz!" I said, dragging him back.

"Take your brats back to your barrack and don't let me find you up here again, understood?"

I returned to our barrack in a mess of tears and blood. We holed up in our little corner and did not move until the food came. My mind was completely numb. I told myself over and over again that I had to react, had to get up, but my body refused to respond. I had to do it for my children. Though I was losing the will to fight, they had their whole lives ahead of them.

"Mom, later on I'll go out and try to find some help. There's got to be someone around here who's willing to help us," Blaz said.

I ran my fingers through his dirty hair and saw something that looked like lice. Within a short time, lice, fleas, and bedbugs would have their way with us. Blaz had always been a good boy, responsible and affectionate. He had eyes only for me. I knew he was capable of doing whatever he could for us, but I was afraid he would get hurt or even killed.

"Don't do anything or go anywhere. This place is very dangerous. We'll think of something. God never abandons his children," I said.

"I think in a place like this we may have to give God a hand," he answered seriously.

I dozed off, and none of the guards bothered me. For a few seconds I dreamed about Johann and our early years of marriage. We were so happy despite the rejection we often encountered. That was why we had moved to Berlin. In the city, nothing seemed to scandalize anyone, certainly not a mixed marriage between an Aryan woman and a Gypsy man. In those days, the mid-1930s, the capital was a hub for all of us trying to shake off the postwar poverty and economic crisis. In our town, after the unexpected return of economic hardships, no one had wanted a Gypsy to have a job that could have gone to a "good German." Many Romani had fought in the Great War. Johann's father had even received the Iron Cross for saving a wounded officer and carrying him from the front to a military hospital, but that did not matter when there was hardly enough work to go around.

Blaz had already been born, and only the good heart of a kind baker married to a Jamaican kept us from starving. She shared her bread with us, which gave me the strength to nurse Blaz and keep our family alive. The Weimar Republic's dream of a more just society had once again devolved into a nightmare.

The memory of Johann bringing a few oranges home was crystal clear. It was Christmas, and all we had to eat that night were some boiled potatoes and two sausages. We sweetened the orange with a sprinkle of sugar. Johann slowly fed little Blaz one slice at a time, laughing as the baby sucked and smacked on the fruit as if it were the most exquisite delicacy on earth.

Constant hunger makes you dream constantly about food. The arrival of lunch brought me back to the reality of camp life. We crawled out of our *koia* for the meager midday ration, which was a very watery, off-putting soup. I gave it all to the children. I had not eaten for three days now, and my strength was starting to wane. I had to find some way to survive or within a few days I would no longer be able to take care of them. Without me, they would not make it even a week.

After the soup, we went out to walk around again. This time, after my encounter with the guard, we avoided the entryway. We walked along the barracks toward the bathrooms. When we passed by number 14, I heard German being spoken. It was the first time I had heard prisoners communicating fluently in our language. I approached cautiously. The children stayed close by me, except for Blaz, who had wanted to walk around on his own.

"Are you German?" I dared to ask two elderly women who were holding babies.

They looked at me with surprise. I was not sure if it was because of my Aryan looks, the cuts on my face, or the passel of children with me. The older one gestured for me to come closer. I leaned down in front of her, and she passed her hand over my face. I began to cry at her gentle touch. The simple show of affection within that inferno was the best gift she could have given me.

"Good God, what have they done to you?" she asked, nearly in a whisper.

"A guard hit me when I went up to the office," I explained.

"Probably the sadist Maria Mandel or Irma Grese, a true beast. They are the worst savages here at Birkenau."

"This place is called Birkenau?" I asked.

"Yes, we're in Birkenau, though it's also called Auschwitz II. But you're not a Gypsy," she said.

I shook my head and said with a heavy voice, "No, but my husband and children are. They wanted to bring them here without me, but I couldn't leave them. I'm their mother."

"And where is your husband?" the other woman asked.

"They separated us when we got here. I think they took him away with a work group," I answered.

The older woman asked, "Was he sick, or very thin?"

Her question puzzled me. "No, strong and healthy as an ox."

"You're sure?" I did not understand her insistence at the time, not until later, when I learned what happened to children, the elderly, and the sick on the other side of the barbed wire.

"So you don't have to worry about him. Those who work get a bit more food and can leave here for the factories," the other woman said.

"Where did they put you with the children?" the older woman asked, her hand still resting on my face.

"In barrack number 4."

"God, no, with the Russians! Those poor brutes have been so mistreated they have nothing human left in them. You've got to get out of there as soon as you can," she replied, clearly startled.

"But how?" The desperation in my voice was clear.

"We'll speak to our barrack supervisor. There are a lot of us here already, but because we're Germans they haven't crammed quite as many in here as in the other barracks. We can find room. She'll make a request to the SS leader. Normally, they accept our requests with no fuss. You'll have to go back to number 4 tonight, but hopefully by tomorrow they'll move you to our barrack. Don't talk to anyone or get into any trouble. Those women are dangerous," she warned.

Her words both depressed and encouraged me. We had had the misfortune of being placed in the worst spot of the Gypsy camp, but it seemed like things might get a little less horrible.

One of the women handed me the baby she was holding, went into the barrack, and came back out with a strip of tape and a bandage. She cleaned my face off with alcohol and covered my wound with the bandage.

"One of our friends is a Polish nurse. She's a Jew. There's not much at the infirmary, but she snuck us a few bandages for the children," she explained.

"I'm a nurse," I volunteered.

"Well, praise heaven. They need all the help they can get at the hospital. There are so few workers and hardly any medicine," she answered.

I stayed talking with the women awhile. It was the first time I had felt human contact since arriving. My crew started playing with some of the children in their barrack. We would have to spend one more night among the horrible company of barrack 4, but someone in Birkenau had finally offered us a shred of help.

When the supervisor from barrack 14 came, she took down my information and gave it to the secretary, who took it to the office. The fact that I was a nurse would grease the wheel for the transfer request. Besides, there was an unwritten rule in the camp that German prisoners received slightly less atrocious treatment than others, unless they were Jews, in which case the treatment was equal.

"We're more fortunate than the poor Jews," the older woman said.

Puzzled by her comment, I asked, "Why do you say that?" I had not yet noticed many luxuries for Gypsies in Auschwitz.

"They're separated as soon as they arrive. The only family camp for Jews is the one for the Czechs. The rest are separated into men and women. Children, mothers, and the elderly disappear. We don't know what they do with them. Maybe they take them to other camps," she explained.

The other old woman frowned and whispered, "Some say they kill them and burn up the bodies."

"Oh, don't say that," the older woman said, crossing herself. "You'll bring us bad *baxt*."

"When they come to shower in the sauna, that's what some of the *Sonderkommandos* have told our men. I think there's a Gypsy among them. They say they burn the bodies in ovens."

"That's just gossip. The Nazis aren't capable of such cruelty. Even that monster Hitler had a mother and a father." The older woman was angry now.

"That son of *Beng*, his only father is Satan," the other woman spat out.

"I can't imagine they've gone to that level," I said. I had seen a lot over the past few years, but human cruelty has its limits—at least I thought so at the time.

We returned to the barrack right before supper, after being allowed a few rushed moments in the bathroom. In silence we ate the piece of black bread and beet compote, and then the younger children went to sleep. They were exhausted. There were too many emotions and not enough food for them to have energy in the late afternoon.

When it got completely dark, Blaz told me what all he had discovered, and I told him about my talk with the older women.

"I learned that the camp to the right of us is the hospital for the whole place," Blaz said. "On the other side is a camp for Jewish men. They leave early every morning to work in the Nazi factories."

"I hope that we'll be transferred to the new barrack tomorrow. I don't think it'll be much better than this one, but at least the people seem nicer." I could not think of any more to say.

Blaz went on with his account. "I've met some kids and I found a little shed near the offices."

I broke in nervously. "Please, no, I told you not to go near there." After the experience from this morning, I knew that being anywhere near the guards or the SS was very dangerous.

"Don't worry, I didn't get close. Just close enough to see the barrack that the SS have behind the storehouse. That's where they go to smoke and drink, and I saw some girls from the camp going in there."

"I don't want you to go back there. It's too dangerous," I warned him.

We fell asleep amidst the groans, complaints, and tossing and turning of the prisoners.

It was again very cold the next morning. The sky was clear, and there was a stiff frost on the ground. The barrack roof hardly offered resistance to the freezing air outside. We got ready quickly, and I hoped desperately that we would be transferred to the German barrack that day. After getting ready and having coffee, we stayed inside. The children were shivering uncontrollably with the cold. Though we tried to warm each other, we hardly had enough calories in our bodies to fight the low temperatures.

One of the more aggressive Russians came up and, pulling out a sort of awl, said, "I need your coats, duchess. My children are cold."

Dubiously, I stood up. I did not want to cause a scene that might jeopardize my chance to leave that barrack, but I could not allow her to have my children's coats.

I held her gaze and spoke calmly. "I wish I could help you, but my children are also cold. Ask for some new ones at the camp office."

Two of the woman's friends came up beside me. Fighting against three women, one of whom was armed, was not a wise move.

Blaz jumped up, slipped between the women, and hurried out of the barrack. They could not stop him, and no one dared go out of the barrack at that hour.

"Where does your snotty-nosed brat think he's going?

They'll bring him back here soon enough black and blue, but that's what your kind deserve—you think bad things never happen to people like you, that it's people like us that deserve all the trouble in this world."

"I don't want any trouble. We're all here unjustly. If we help each other, we can make it through, but if we act like animals, the Nazis will do away with us in the blink of an eye," I tried to explain.

The woman raised the awl and started moving it back and forth. I followed her movements with my eyes then took off my coat and rolled it around my right arm. Johann had showed me what Gypsies did in a knife fight. The Russian woman looked at me with surprise, as if having second thoughts, but she kept threatening us. It was three on one, and they knew I would not last long.

Behind me, the children were crying. Only Otis stayed calm. He had come up beside me, as if he could help me fight the three wild animals.

The rest of the prisoners and their children formed a semicircle around us, not wanting to miss any of the action. My heart was racing. The little bit of vitality I had left flushed intensely in that moment, to help me take these women on. I could not allow them to humiliate me again. The coats were the only thing standing between my children and certain death.

"If you won't give them up easily, it'll have to be the hard way," the woman said, making a first attempt to stab me.

I managed to dodge and hit her in the stomach with my other arm. She bent over in pain, but the other two women jumped on me and yanked my hair, dragging me down to the muddy floor. The first woman seized her chance and sat hard on my chest, pressing the awl to my throat. Otis hit at one of the women, but one push was enough to send him flying into the *koia*.

"Your brats are going to be left motherless, but that hardly matters. They were going to die sooner or later. People like you don't survive long in a place like this."

I tried to sit up, but the other two women were pinning my arms down. I thought about begging, but it would have made no difference. The poor Russian women were hardly more than savage beasts.

Just then Blaz showed up in the doorway, followed by several men and women. Gypsies from barrack 14 had come en masse to help us.

"Russians, leave the *Gadje* alone!" shouted the old woman I had met the day before.

My three assailants stood up defiantly, but when they saw the dozen men and women armed with knives, awls, and other homemade weapons, they merely stepped aside and let the Germans come toward me.

"Get your things. They've already given you clearance to move into our barrack," the old woman said, smiling. She looked around and spat out, "This woman is untouchable, you hear me? If you even think about getting close to her or trying to hurt her, we won't stop 'til you're all dead. Understood?"

Her words had the desired effect on the Russians. I gathered our few remaining possessions and left the barrack with the children clinging to me. The German Gypsies surrounded us like a personal escort and took us back to their barrack, with no kapos interfering. Apparently they held significant sway in the camp and no one messed with them. The old woman showed me the *koia* where we could sleep. This barrack was a slight step up from the others. They kept it cleaner, and there were fewer prisoners here. It was no paradise, but at least it was less of an inferno than our first hours in Auschwitz.

After I put our things in our new area, I noticed that my vision was growing blurry. Before I could sit down, I slumped to the floor. When I came to, several women were around me, while others were comforting my children.

The old woman had my head in her lap, and when she saw my eyes open, she asked how long it had been since I had eaten. She held a sausage of some sort out to me. I took a few bites—it was just going bad—but then I shook my head and said she should give it to the children.

"We'll get them something in a minute, but if you don't eat, they won't have a mother to take care of them, and they'll be sent to barrack 16, where the orphans go. Those poor babies don't last long."

I ate the rest of the sausage slowly, savoring it like a succulent delicacy. It had been several days since any solid food had passed my lips. Very soon I felt a bit of strength returning. I sat up a little and looked at my children. They were playing with another child in the barrack. They seemed calmer and less fearful than before.

"You'll all be fine here. We've got no luxuries, but we help each other out. Tomorrow you'll start work at the hospital. The doctors were very pleased to learn that there was a new nurse at the camp." The old woman smiled as she spoke.

That was music to my ears. In a place like Auschwitz, having a role to play might be the one thing that saved you from a certain death.

"Where will the children go while I work?" I asked her, suddenly anxious again.

"Don't worry, we'll watch them. We've got plenty of sick in our midst. You'll pay us back in time with your care," she answered.

"What's your name?" I asked. She had never volunteered the information.

"Anna, Anna Rosenberg, though many just call me *Oma*."

That night I slept decently for the first time since we had been forced out of our apartment. Somehow, the merest breath of hope had returned. Now I was part of a community, and they would help protect me. My main concern then became my husband's whereabouts. I had had no news of him since we were separated upon arrival to the camp. Some women had told me it was very difficult to make contact with anyone outside of our camp, but I did not want to give up on the idea.

Sometimes, when reality scrapes against your heart, it is better to avoid it with daydreams. Thus, when I closed my eyes, I tried to imagine how our life would be when all this was over. Johann would return to the Philharmonic, our children would go to college, and we would buy a small house on the outskirts of Berlin. When our grandchildren were born, we would play with them beside the warm hearth while the snow fell gently outside and blanketed the world in a delicious white.

FIVE

MAY 1943
AUSCHWITZ

Of all that I dreamed about during those long nights of watching and waiting, the only thing that came true was the blanket of snow that covered all the Birkenau mud. No one expected it at the end of May, but there it was nonetheless, harvesting a good number of defenseless lives now freed forever from pain and suffering, thanks to the lady in white. The work ahead in the following weeks was exhausting. Several of the long-staying veterans who had once lived in the quarters of the Polish army at Auschwitz I told me the sign over the gate leading into the camp—*Arbeit macht frei*—read "Work sets you free." Every day, dozens of people passed through the hospital, most dying within two or three days. The members of the health-care team did not have the medicine, surgical equipment, or pain relief necessary to adequately treat the invalids.

I worked with a Polish nurse named Ludwika and under Dr. Senkteller. The nurse was Jewish and had suffered through several ghettos before landing at the camp. Her face reflected better than any other I encountered the insensitivity one was at risk of contracting in Auschwitz. Dr. Senkteller apparently had not given up yet, fighting with the camp for access to medicine and better treatment for his poor patients. Both of them were excellent professionals and people, but without surgical equipment or medicine, they could do little to fight the rampant gangrene, typhus, malaria, dysentery, and diarrhea, given the deplorable hygiene and diet allowed the prisoners. Typhus was a serious concern at the camp. The number of cases had multiplied, especially since the arrival of a party of Czech Gypsies. The only way to prevent the spread of the disease was to completely disinfect the barracks. The new medical chief of staff, Dr. Mengele, had proposed the measure.

For some time we had been working under the supervision of Dr. Wirths, but Birkenau was bursting at the seams, and they had sent new doctors from Berlin. Wirths, the chief doctor, was from an entire family of doctors. While he always put on a good face to calm his guinea pigs, he rarely showed anything like humanity. Dr. Senkteller told me that one time Wirths, in the presence of Dr. Senkteller's brother Edward, had operated on a patient without administering anesthesia. The Auschwitz patient had several malignant tumors, and the chief doctor was torturing the dying man without the least sign of compassion. Patients often had panic attacks when they saw us approaching in our white aprons. For them, we were nothing less than the essence of pain and drawn-out suffering.

The medical team at the *Zigeunerfamilienlager* talked of little but the new arrival in charge of the hospital. Dr. Mengele was a young man just over thirty years old who had been injured on the Russian front. The first time I saw him, he struck me as a handsome, polite, agreeable man. He was always smiling, especially with the children. He did not seem like the other Nazis in Auschwitz who, with their gray or black uniforms, looked like death lords harvesting the fields of Poland with their scythes.

Yet the new sanitary measures of the new chief doctor at the *Zigeunerfamilienlager* could not have been more extreme. By the end of May, the barracks were disinfected as prescribed. I oversaw the process for barrack 14, where my children and I were living then. Those were particularly difficult days in the camp. The cold in Birkenau was a very humid cold. Once it seeped into the marrow of your bones, nothing could stop your shaking.

That freezing morning, the kapos and scribes were charged with driving all the prisoners out of the barracks. Families ran hither and yon half-dressed, as the guards had not allowed anyone to take anything out of the *koia*. First, prisoners were forced to completely strip down. Then, on threat of beating, they were forced to get into a tub with disinfectant that burned their skin. I recall one woman, Ana, who was carrying a baby. The naked body of the child was pink with cold, but they did not allow her to cover the baby. She begged and pleaded, and finally one of the guards yanked the baby out of her hands. The poor thing was hardly moving, half-frozen from the cold and sluggish from weakness. The guard plunged the creature into the disinfectant and, after he came out half-drowned and with his skin on fire, she handed him back to his mother. The mother screamed in pain while the child died in her arms.

The guards and kapos did not care if the prisoners were elderly, women, or children: everyone had to be disinfected. And right after, they shaved their hair and beards. Then the prisoners were left to stand naked in the snow until they were allowed entrance into the bathroom to tidy up and get dressed. The barracks were disinfected, but within days they were once again a breeding ground for parasites. The cruel, brutal disinfection had been for naught.

A few days later, on May 25, when there were new cases

of typhus, Dr. Mengele called all the doctors and nurses together in barrack 28, where all the medical staff lived except for me. I continued living in barrack 14 with my children. After the first few days of his interventions, we had all learned to fear the SS official. Mengele stood with his fists on his hips and a frown on his face, saying, "Typhus is back, and barracks 9, 10, 11, 12, and 13 are infected. We can't allow the epidemic to spread. The recent disinfection measures have not produced the desired effect. Therefore, I have given orders to eliminate all the members of barracks 8 through 14."

Our jaws dropped. We were horrified at Mengele's words. The suffering of the past few days of disinfection had been worthless. What did he mean by *eliminate*? What would happen to the prisoners of all those barracks? No one spoke up. Extremely aware that one word might mean immediate death, no one dared contradict an SS officer.

When he finished speaking, Mengele turned his back to indicate the meeting was over. One by one, my colleagues left the room, but I stayed put, waiting until I was alone with him. Ludwika tugged my white blouse to get me to leave, but I stayed where I was.

Mengele finally turned and saw me standing there, my head down. He cleared his throat, impatient to hear what I had to say.

"Herr Doktor . . ."

"What do you want? Your number is . . . ?"

"I'm the nurse, Helene Hannemann. My parents are German, and I studied at the University of Berlin."

"You're German? Then you're a Jew?"

"No, Herr Doktor. I'm Aryan, as is my entire family."

"Then you're a political prisoner?"

"No, I'm here to take care of my children. My husband is a Gypsy, and the police thought my children should be brought here, but I could not allow them to remain without their mother," I said.

"I'm sorry, I don't have time for moving personal stories. I'm here to keep the camp from going extinct. The plague of typhus will do us all in within a matter of weeks if we don't take drastic measures."

The doctor seemed to intuit what I was going to ask. Despite his affable mannerisms and his wide smile, he was nothing less than the ferocious SS officer his uniform proclaimed him to be.

"You've said that you'll eliminate all the members of barracks 8 through 14. That's over fifteen hundred innocent people." My voice was trembling.

"A minor inconvenience. Otherwise, over twenty thousand Gypsies throughout the camp will die," he answered dryly.

"Barracks 8 and 14 aren't infected . . ." My words faltered.

"But due to their close proximity to those that are, there are very likely cases of the disease," he said. It seemed as if he was tiring of the conversation.

"If there were a new outbreak, you could eliminate those barracks," I said.

"It's out of the question. Much better to prevent than to treat. The laws of war are harsh. In times like these, we all have to make sacrifices. You've no idea what I've had to put up with on the Russian front. This place is paradise on earth in comparison." He shook his head with disgust.

I was sweating then. He seemed completely unwilling to listen to me, and I had already risked too much. My life meant absolutely nothing to him. He could do away with me with the stroke of a pen, and that in a very steady hand.

He was impatient. "What's the problem? Do you have family members in those barracks?"

"Yes, my children are in barrack 14," I said, hesitating. He might use the information against me.

"Well, we'll take your children out of the barrack if that's what's worrying you. Are you happy now? You can go." He dismissed me dryly.

I remained standing. The German took two steps forward, his black boots slapping against the wooden floor.

He came so close to my face that I could smell his cologne. I had not inhaled anything so pleasant in weeks.

"And now what do you want?" he asked with a furrowed brow and twisted mouth.

"I'm begging you to spare barracks 8 and 14, Herr Doktor. It would be criminal to kill all those innocent people." I couldn't believe the words had come out of my mouth. I had just signed my death sentence.

He looked at me, startled. The word *criminal* seemed to anger him, but he calmed himself before answering. I imagined that no one had spoken to him like that, much less a prisoner. I do not know if my saving graces were my Aryan looks or the bravery of my actions, but the fact is that Mengele bent over the table, wrote a note, and handed it to me.

"Barracks 8 and 14 will be spared. If there is even one case of typhus, I will eliminate them immediately, understood? I'm not doing this for you. I just want you to understand I don't enjoy any of this. We have to sacrifice the weak so the strong can survive. The only way for nature to stay the course is for us to let her choose who should live and who should die."

"Yes, Herr Doktor," I answered, trembling, though I tried to steady my pulse when he handed me the paper signed with his fountain pen.

"Take this letter to the secretary, Guttenberger. She won't have processed the order yet," he said.

"Thank you," I said.

"Don't thank me, Frau Hannemann. My job here is to save the camp and do my duties, not to cater to the lives of the inmates. Germany is keeping thousands of non-Aryans alive, but it won't do so for free or by tending to absurd humanitarian concerns," he answered arrogantly.

I got out of the barrack as quickly as I could and nearly ran to the office. I did not want the revised order to arrive too late. I was out of breath by the time I arrived. One of the Nazi guards, Maria Mandel, approached. The wound I had received at her hand right after we arrived at Auschwitz was still not fully healed.

"Where do you think you're going, Gypsy slut?" she asked, whip raised.

"I have orders from Dr. Mengele." I held out the paper.

She made as if to crumple it up and throw it away, but another guard appeared behind her. Irma Grese hissed, "Are you looking for trouble? Don't you recognize Mengele's signature on that?"

Mandel frowned. She checked the signature and allowed me to go through.

Barely daring to breathe, I entered the main room and left the paper on the desk of Elisabeth Guttenberger. She was a smart, beautiful Gypsy. We had hardly exchanged a handful of words, but most prisoners spoke well of her. Her family had sold antiques and stringed instruments in Stuttgart. Her father had been a deputy in the Reichstag and one of the most renowned members of the Gypsy community.

"Dr. Mengele has halted the elimination of barracks 8 and 14," I said, still trying to catch my breath.

"Thank God for that at least. When I saw the order, my blood turned cold," Elisabeth said, sealing the paper.

"I'm so sorry for all who will die tomorrow," I replied.

"The one sure thing here is that we're all going to die. But if we can save anyone, our daily struggles will have been worth it," Elisabeth answered. "I've been here since the middle of March, and all I've seen is death and desolation. They arrested my entire family in Munich. Several of my brothers and sisters are here in the camp, and I try to use my position to help them, but it's almost pointless. There's nothing to share around."

"At least you've got a decent job now," I said.

"When we got here, we had to build the barracks and the streets of the camp. My father couldn't handle the pace of the work, and he was the first to die. Who knows how many of us will make it out of here alive? Sometimes I think none of us will."

Her words drove home once again the inexorable reality of Auschwitz. Delaying the deaths of a few was pointless if we were all going to die here.

Mandel's entrance put an abrupt end to the conversation. That fearsome woman could crack your soul with a simple glance. I never could understand how the guards had achieved such an advanced degree of dehumanization. I finally just accepted the fact that they saw us as beasts they had to watch over and exterminate if necessary. I walked back to my barrack slowly, taking a deep breath before entering. I let it out slowly as I entered and saw all the German Gypsies. If I had gotten to the office a few minutes later, all of these people would have been killed the next day.

My children ran to me when they saw me come in. Blaz gave me a detailed report of the day, as he was charged with taking care of his younger siblings. That day, Otis had gotten into a fight with another child, but Blaz had separated them. And the twins had stolen the crutches of an elderly gentleman, Klaus, but it was just a marvelous joke to them all. Finally, Adalia had behaved herself very well, as usual. She had hardly left Anna's side all day, and Anna treated her like her own granddaughter.

I handed out the food I had been able to sneak that day. In my position as a nurse, it was somewhat easier to come

69

upon a bit of bread, potatoes, and cans of sardines. It was not much, but every day I delivered it to a different family in the barrack. Then I sat for a while to talk with Anna.

She asked, "You okay? You look particularly down in the dumps."

"It's been a very difficult day," I said. I didn't want to elaborate.

"Aren't they all? Every day here is an uphill climb."

"True." I nodded absently.

"We know already," she added in a softer tone, trying to avoid being overheard. The camp was like a small town. News spread like wildfire.

"I couldn't do anything for them." I shook my head in despair.

"But you were able to for us. Sooner or later, they'd kill them anyhow. Sick people don't last long here. And we don't always accomplish what we set out to do in life. I was raised in Frankfurt. As far back as we can remember, my family has been boilermakers. We made a good living, but every so often we'd get kicked out of a town because somebody lost something, or there were some robberies. In a little town outside of Frankfurt I met a teacher named Maria. She was an angel. With her big heart, one day she went up and asked my father to let her teach me how to read and write. My father said he needed me to work in the factory but that if she could teach me in the evenings and on Sundays, he didn't mind. I learned how to read and write within a month. I was already thirteen years old, but I had a quick mind and boundless curiosity. But then a family brought us their son and arranged a marriage."

"At thirteen?" I asked, incredulous. For quite a while now marriage before sixteen had been illegal.

"Yes, well, they waited until I turned fourteen, but my mother didn't let me go to school after that. I had to learn how to cook, sew, and do other things more suitable for women."

"How sad," I said.

She shrugged. "It's okay. I suffered a great deal with my husband, but I had five wonderful children. I made sure they all went to school, including the girls, but it hasn't amounted to much. The Nazis have destroyed so much."

"Well, thanks to what you learned, you were able to give your children an education. You've managed to keep the German Gypsies united in this camp, and you saved my family. I admire you, Anna. I haven't known many women as brave as you."

The old woman's eyes grew misty for a moment. We all tried to stay calm for the sake of the children, but sometimes it was impossible to control our feelings.

Anna was a very wise woman. She led the German

Gypsies in peaceful living, making sure everyone took care of everyone else like in a big family. I rested my head against her shoulder for a moment. I felt like I had stood up to evil and won that day. Dr. Mengele was the perfect combination of indifference and efficiency. He knew that it was not a good idea to go against everyone in the Gypsy camp, but he wanted his superiors to approve of his work. That was his weak spot. Unlike the rest of the members of the SS, he was capable of giving in, if he thought that by doing so he could improve his esteem in the eyes of his superiors or gain the assistance of his subordinates in carrying out his vision.

When dinner arrived, I went to my children. They were better off than they had been a couple weeks before, but they were still dirtier and skinnier by the day. If they got sick, I knew there was little I could do to save them. And they were the only hope keeping me alive. I hugged them tight. Feeling their slender bodies next to mine, I yearned with all my strength for them to enter my womb again, to be part of a deeper oneness with them in the perfect symbiosis between mother and child. That night I had saved their lives once again. Perhaps I had been unknowingly selfish. One day more in Auschwitz meant drawing out the agony of death, keeping the soul captive behind the cruel bars of our executioners' indifference.

The smiles of my children made me forget for a moment

the torment of the recent weeks. I did not want to think about what would happen tomorrow. Over a thousand people would lose their lives at the whim of one doctor. But for him—for all of them—we were nothing more than animals to be sacrificed for a higher ideal. Curse the ideals that make humans vile! Mothers have no ideologies. Our children are our only cause, our fatherland. For men, killing and dying for ideas may come naturally. For us bearers of life, to murder for ideals is the worst aberration created by humankind. Mothers capable of generating life could never become accomplices to so much death.

SIX

MAY 1943
AUSCHWITZ

The next morning, none of us were allowed out of the barracks to go to the bathroom. Doctors and nurses, though, were required to be outside. The SS knew they needed us to help the poor wretches who were going to be eliminated that day think that they really were being transferred to a hospital to treat their typhus. Mengele showed up in a black convertible as if he were on his way to a picnic on this mild sunny day instead of to an indiscriminate slaughter. A few minutes later, half a dozen dark-green trucks with SS guards came down the central avenue for the rapid loading of all the prisoners from barracks 9 through 13. They looked like carrion vultures scavenging for their daily ration of meat.

The soldiers, faces covered by antiseptic masks, stood

in front of the first two barracks and asked the Gypsies to file out in order. They tried to be as amenable as possible to decrease resistance. We stayed in line beside Dr. Mengele, who hummed ceaselessly while the army of desperate souls passed us by. First came the strongest, the men and elderly who were perhaps not yet infected but had the misfortune of living in the wrong barrack. Then came the invalids. Some prisoners brought the weakest of their group out on makeshift cots, and these were piled into the trucks like logs, tumbled one on top of the other with no thought to the extreme care needed by the sick.

I could not watch the disgraceful spectacle. I knew I had managed to save a few hundred people, but I felt like an accomplice to the murder of the others. One mother came out holding her children by the hands. The three little ones stared at us with eyes bulging from hunger and fever. One lurched toward us, but the guards—covered in masks and gloves—put him back in line.

There were more scenes of panic in the last barrack. By then the rumor had surely reached them that they were being sent to certain death. Several attempted unsuccessful escapes or threw themselves at Dr. Mengele's feet to plead for their lives. He, meanwhile, just kept humming until all the prisoners had been loaded onto the trucks going who knows where, yet wherever it was held imminent death.

"Now it's your turn. You all get to the hospital and pick out everyone infected with typhus. We can't leave a single focal point of the disease in the camp." Mengele smiled at us as he spoke.

A chill ran up my spine. The doctors would do the selecting, but we nurses would have to be present and take the invalids to the exit and hand them over to the soldiers. First we went through the men's hospital barrack. Some twenty were chosen, among whom was a child Otis's age. The young thing had barely started his walk of life and within a few minutes would be snuffed out forever. The women's hospital barrack held even more dramatic scenes, as several of the women had their babies with them.

One of the women, a dark young Gypsy with huge green eyes, tugged on my uniform and whispered, "The child isn't sick. Please, take care of her."

I looked at Mengele, who was caught up discussing with Dr. Senkteller the case of two elderly women who may or may not have had typhus. I took the child wrapped in her clean white blanket—something rarely seen in the camp—and carried her to the back of the room. I put her in one of the empty cribs. It might cost me my job or even my life, but I was a mother. I knew what that young girl felt as she pleaded for her baby.

The disinfection routine was repeated until the last

barrack was empty and the last typhus patient had been loaded onto the SS trucks. When the Nazis drove away, camp life went back to business as usual, but a shadow of terror covered everything a bit more darkly than usual. Who would be next? Human life meant nothing in this infernal place.

I was free the rest of the morning, as I had asked for permission to be with my children. I needed to embrace them and get through that horrible experience in their presence. The purge of the invalids had left me speechlessly depressed.

By the afternoon I had to return to the hospital. Dr. Mengele showed up unexpectedly and called everyone in to another meeting. It was odd for him to be there at that hour, as recently he had been assigned to make selections of new arrivals on the train platform. We knew that whatever he was going to share could not be good, but at least we were allowed to know what to expect, whereas the rest of the prisoners were completely at his mercy, ignorant of what the next day might hold.

I walked down the main avenue beside Ludwika. She seemed as depressed as I was as we approached the medical barracks.

"I don't know how much longer I can take it. I thought I'd get used to it, but since Dr. Mengele showed up, it's just gotten worse," she said, on the verge of tears.

"You think so? He may be more dramatic than his predecessor, but at least we know what he's after. If we could convince him that improvements to the camp would further his career, I think things would get a lot better." I was trying to cheer her up.

"You think personal ambition is any easier to manage than fanaticism? I think Mengele is the marriage of the two."

"Well, let's not get ahead of ourselves," I said as we climbed the steps.

A dozen people were inside the barrack, two of whom I had never seen before.

"My dear colleagues, allow me to introduce you to a new acquisition for the team, Dr. Zosia Ulewicz. She'll be my personal assistant in the laboratory I'm going to open behind the sauna. And Berthold Epstein is a renowned pediatrician who will help us treat the children. You're already aware that we receive the inestimable support of the Kaiser Wilhelm Institute of Berlin, especially from its director, von Verschuer. We have to do our jobs very well to continue receiving his help. I hope you are all willing to work hard. Don't forget you are among the privileged here in Birkenau," Mengele said with all seriousness. His intimidating voice produced a long silence.

The doctor took a piece of paper from his desk and waved it in our faces.

"You did not do your jobs well this morning. I had been assured that there were no cases of typhus in barrack 8, but this very afternoon I myself have diagnosed two cases. Do you know what this means? I am forced to empty another barrack. If you had done your jobs well, things like this would not have to happen."

His words petrified us. We had thought the worst of the purge was over, but in Auschwitz, things never happened logically. Every day was completely unpredictable.

"Tomorrow we will eliminate barrack 8, and I hope I don't have to do away with the entire Gypsy camp because of you lot. Can you imagine how it would displease Dr. Robert Ritter if his Gypsy colony were exterminated? You know how the professor loves his theories of Aryan origin, especially about the Gypsies, who have remained purebreds since their arrival from India," he droned on, his rage only building.

We were shell-shocked. The camp was completely terrified, and many of us felt we were the cause of their misfortune. Mengele was astute in passing the blame on to those around him. While his drastic measures made him stand out in the eyes of Dr. Wirths, we were the ones who had to choose who would live and who would die among the hospital's inmates.

Mengele dismissed us all with a thoughtless wave. He

cared nothing for how we felt. He was only interested in our efficiency in getting the job done. I was walking out the door when his soft voice paralyzed me.

"Nurse Hannemann, please stay for a moment."

Ludwika threw me a worried glance. It was not a good sign that the doctor would want to talk to me alone. I started trembling as I took baby steps toward him. I worried that the decision to spare barrack 8 would now come back to haunt me, but I was ready to face the consequences. My only concern was for my children, though I knew Anna would take care of them if something happened to me.

"I imagine this whole situation will have put you on edge. I've looked into your case. I needed to clear up a few matters. Your racial purity is enviable; your parents are active in their community, though to their disgrace they are not registered members of the party. You must think I'm a monster, but, I can assure you, that is far from the truth. I have only tried to act in a logical, efficient manner. You have realized by now that resources are very limited in Auschwitz and illnesses abound. I imagine you do not approve of my method of containing the plague of typhus, but I am only letting nature make her choice: the weakest must die and the strongest survive." He driveled on with his pseudoscientific speech.

I stayed silent, my head lowered. I knew he did not like

direct eye contact, especially from prisoners. Unexpectedly, I felt his fingers touch my chin and push my face upward.

"I admire your courage," he went on. "I do not understand why you would sacrifice yourself for mixed-blood children or why you married a Gypsy, but facing all of this of your own free will . . . With your attitude, you have demonstrated admirable poise, which is why I think you are the ideal candidate. Many of the Gypsy prisoners respect and admire you. Your superiors tell me you have organizational gifts and know how to maintain discipline. This is why I want you to be the director of the nursery and school I'm going to open in Auschwitz-Birkenau. I don't want the twins and the Gypsy children to suffer so many hardships."

At first I had no idea what he was talking about. I could not fathom that it would occur to anyone to open a nursery or school in Auschwitz. In the little time I had been at the concentration camp, I had observed only desolation and death. Why would Dr. Mengele want to do this? I suspected the altruism of his motivations. He did not strike me as generous or sentimental. His practical character allowed little compassion for anyone who was not Aryan.

"You want me to run a children's school here?" I asked, trying to comprehend his words. It sounded like a macabre joke. How could we take care of children in these conditions? What could we offer them?

"Yes, that's exactly what I'm asking. I'll bring you all the supplies you need, food, new clothes, milk, children's films. At least they won't have to suffer like the rest of the internees."

"I'll think about it," I said, unsure how to respond.

"I'll await your answer by tomorrow noon," he said, smiling. He knew I had no way of refusing his request.

I was walking through a mental fog as I made my way back to my barrack. I might be able to do something actually helpful for the camp's children and save my own brood at the same time. I had no idea what was behind Mengele's sudden change of heart, but I could not refuse. The children came first.

When I got to barrack 14 and saw them all running around on stick-thin legs covered by filthy clothes, I started daydreaming about the children's school. I would make sure it was the best thing to ever happen in a concentration camp. Finally, I started to understand why fate had brought me to Auschwitz. I could see the pieces fitting together: being separated from my husband, those most wretched first few days—perhaps it would not all have been for naught. Now I could bring a bit of hope to the Gypsy camp at Birkenau. I could keep as many children alive as possible until the horrible war was over.

Johann had told me once that he had heard Himmler

say on the radio that, after the war, all the Gypsies would be relocated to a reservation where they could live according to their ancestral customs without interference. It all sounded like castles in the air, but that day I could at least start dreaming. I had now been given the sacred mission of saving the Gypsy children at Birkenau, which would start by reviving their will to live in the midst of all that death.

SEVEN

MAY 1943
AUSCHWITZ

The first person I went to for advice was Anna. Besides being a wise old woman and having a big heart, she was also sharp as a tack and impossible to manipulate. In Auschwitz, it was hard to think clearly. Our feelings were under constant anesthesia, yet the atmosphere was simultaneously asphyxiating and kept us from seeing things with any degree of perspective.

I approached her in the brief, peaceful moments of the afternoon when she typically sat at the barrack doorway. She turned her endlessly loving smile on me. Her deep, glassy eyes set off by ravines of wrinkles seemed to intuit what I needed.

"What's on your mind?" she asked before I said a word.

"The past couple days have been particularly difficult for me. Besides the elimination of the barracks, the SS have required us to select the prisoners infected with typhus so they can be removed from the camp. No one has told us what will happen to them, but we all know they aren't being transferred to the camp hospital. They disappear on trucks and none of them come back alive from wherever they're taken." I let it all spill out quickly.

Anna's answer was soft. "Many have died, and many more will die. The Nazis didn't bring us here to take care of us. The only thing they want is to control us, and if we bother them, they'll kill us. I don't want you to harbor any illusions, even though you, being German, have a slightly less abysmal probability of surviving. To those racists, we're nothing but brute animals; yet they see you as an Aryan who's lost her mind by coming to this camp with her Gypsy children."

I appreciated Anna's ability to hold both optimism and realism in tension. She did not allow herself to be fooled as many other prisoners did. After a certain age, life can no longer surprise or confuse you all the way. Gypsies had been persecuted since they had arrived in Europe five hundred years before. Kingdoms, empires, and legal systems had tried to exterminate or assimilate them, yet while governments rose and fell, Gypsies kept doing as they had done for nearly half a millennium.

I could not hold back my news any longer. "Dr. Mengele has offered me the opportunity to start and run a children's school here at the camp."

She nodded, seemingly unsurprised. The idea sounded preposterous, like another bad joke for the Nazis to laugh at us, yet she hardly batted an eye. She just looked at me and said, "Well, what are you waiting for? Nothing worse can happen to these children than what's already happened. At least they'll have somewhere to play, to hide out and forget about this hellhole for a while. From the first time I saw you, I knew God had brought you here to ease our pain somehow. You were so lost, confused, and scared, but I could see a fierce determination in the back of your eyes."

I answered with a hug and started to cry. For the first time since we arrived in Auschwitz, my tears were not out of desperation, rage, or fear; rather, the tension of the last few days had pummeled my heart. I had never known that having someone else's life or death in your hands was even worse than feeling your own perilous position. I did not trust Dr. Mengele. Ever since he came, things at the camp had gotten even worse, but perhaps we could somehow leverage his vanity to help the rest of the prisoners. It was a risky game, but I was willing to try. The children would have somewhere to be that was clean, dry, and warm. They would get better food, and their outlook would brighten. It was worth a shot.

Though I had mostly made up my mind, I decided to go to the barrack where the doctors and nurses slept, to talk with Ludwika. She had been at Auschwitz longer than I and knew what it was like to work with the SS. She could give me a second opinion before I made my final decision.

When I went up the stairs and entered their door, I was surprised by the relatively decent conditions my colleagues lived in. Naturally, there were no luxuries, but they had beds with mattresses, sheets, and clean blankets, a table to eat at, and a small wood-burning stove in what served as a living room. Besides, they were eating foods that the rest of the prisoners hardly dared dream about anymore.

One of the new doctors, Zosia, Mengele's assistant, was reading a medical text by candlelight. Books were another privilege reserved only for doctors.

"Do you know where Ludwika is?" I asked.

The Jewish doctor pulled her eyes away from the book for a moment and, somewhat annoyed, said in perfect German, "Was it your idea to save the baby? She's been here in the barrack with us for two days now. If the SS decide to come poking around, they'll kill us all. Dr. Mengele made it very clear that everyone with typhus or who had been in contact with a typhus patient had to be eliminated.

Ludwika's got the baby in our room. She's alone almost all day until we get back in the afternoon. Anyone could hear her crying. Get that brat out of here ASAP."

I had not expected that reaction. I did not blame Zosia for being afraid—I was too—but in all my interactions with Jewish medical staff up to then, I had detected a deep love for life and the determination to do everything they could for their patients. Ludwika came out of their room when she heard us speaking. She was carrying the baby. Frowning, she went up to Zosia and put the child in her lap.

"Fine, take her to the SS. You know what they'll do with her. Isn't that what you want? None of us may get out of here alive, but I'm not going to let the Nazis destroy my soul. As long as I've got an ounce of humanity left in me, I'm going to risk my life for others."

The Polish nurse's words seemed to get through to the doctor. Holding the child in her arms, she dropped her head and started to weep. Then she pressed the child tightly to her chest and started rocking back and forth, whispering a name. Ludwika and I stared at her, perplexed at what we were witnessing.

"My baby—they took him from me when I came to Auschwitz." Zosia spoke so softly we had to lean forward to hear. "They ripped him out of my hands. They let me live because I'm a doctor, but my baby boy was eliminated.

So when I saw this one, I just kept asking over and over, why does this baby get to live and mine doesn't? I'm so, so angry. But she's just a tiny baby. She didn't do anything. A sweet little helpless newborn. Good God, how long will this nightmare last?"

She continued rocking back and forth, rocking out her pain with the child, until Ludwika gently took the baby and hushed her to sleep.

"I can take the baby. The doctor is right; if they find the child here, it'll only cause problems. But there are dozens of children in our barrack, so the guards won't notice another one. Besides, I've decided to accept the job of running the camp nursery school," I added with a smile.

The two women stared at me in surprise. First, because it was highly unusual to see someone smile in Auschwitz. Only children and guards were allowed that luxury, though the malicious grins of the guards and the SS were poisoned with a mixture of indifference and disdain.

"A nursery school in Auschwitz?" Ludwika asked in disbelief.

"Yes, a nursery and school with swings, painted walls, cartoons, food, milk, and everything that children need," I answered with heady glee.

Every time I said the words out loud, I felt a new rush of euphoria as I started to actually believe it might happen.

I could see in my mind's eye how we would decorate the place, the crayons, the notebooks, the blackboard and chalk. The children would have a full glass of milk for breakfast while we read stories that would help them forget where we were.

Ludwika could not recover from the shock. "But who has authorized it?"

"Dr. Mengele. A few hours ago he asked me to consider it," I said.

Now Zosia chimed in with renewed incredulity, "It was Dr. Mengele who came up with this idea?"

"Yes, the man himself. I could not believe the Germans would do something like that in this place." I was beaming, no longer holding back the hope that surged through me.

Yet my two colleagues were less than enthusiastic. I chalked it up to their long stay in Auschwitz. The camp was capable of emptying the world's most loving heart.

Ludwika asked, "What answer did you give him?"

"I haven't answered anything yet. I wanted to get your opinion."

She shrugged, the child still in her arms, and said in a serious tone, "My opinion doesn't matter. The children would have a better life, and I think that's reason enough to accept. I'll help you as much as I can with whatever you need."

I went and hugged her. Zosia studied me from her chair, and I could see fear in her eyes. I presumed that for a mother who had just lost her baby it must be difficult to hear of other children getting to go to a nursery. Then I took the baby from Ludwika and asked for her things. I would take her back to our barrack that night.

"I wanted one more night with her, but it's better for you to go ahead and take her. It's a bad idea to love anyone in this place. Everything you try to hold on to in this camp disappears. Better not to have any attachments." Ludwika had steeled her face.

She went to their room and got the baby's few things. She handed me a knapsack with a few diapers, some clothes, an old rattle, and a blanket.

"Thank you both so much for your support. I'm impatient to see Mengele tomorrow and give him my answer," I said, leaving the barrack.

I was not one to get swept up in wishful thinking, but I must admit that that night, for the first time since our arrival in Birkenau, I felt something resembling happiness. My feet walked lightly down the muddy road, and when I showed up in barrack 14 with the baby in my arms, a group of women huddled around me. It was amazing to see how even in that place, a newborn caused the same reaction as anywhere else, a mix of tenderness and love.

My children crowded around to look at the child. Eventually Adalia opened her eyes wide and asked, "Did you have another baby? Is this my new little sister?"

All the women burst out laughing, though the idea did not sit well with the twins. They crossed their arms and huffed.

"No, sweetie, this baby doesn't have a mama, and we're going to take care of her for a while," I answered.

Anna took the baby and started to rock her. Little by little the crowd went back to their *koias*.

"I'll keep her with me tonight. You need to rest," the old woman said.

"Are you sure?" It was not easy to sleep with a baby. Anna was already quite old, and the camp had depleted her strength a great deal.

"It will be a joy to feel a baby's skin against me again. I had five of my own. I saw three of them die, and I hope I don't survive the others. The only family I've got left with me now is Fremont, my youngest grandson. They caught us as we fled to Slovakia. We had family there, but some peasants reported us to the soldiers near the front. A few more hours and we would've been out of reach of this nightmare. Two of my sons managed to escape in the confusion when they took us to an improvised camp where they were rounding up all the Jews, Gypsies, and homosexuals. Then they packed us on a train and sent us to Auschwitz I. They let us keep our clothes, but they shaved our heads when we got there. Life was a little less terrible there than here. The buildings were made of brick, which at least kept out a little of the cold. But at the end of March they brought us here, and we joined the prisoners who were finishing up building the barracks. We had the misfortune of being among the first occupants." The sadness on Anna's face took my breath away.

When someone's feelings surfaced, we all seemed to crack. The only way to survive was to try to think as little as possible and numb your feelings.

The children and I went to our bed. The three little ones surrounded me like newborn chicks burrowing into the mother hen. The two older ones stayed just a bit farther, anxious to tell me about their adventures from the day, though they knew they should wait until the younger ones were asleep.

"Today has been so interesting," Otis said very seriously. Sometimes his posture, the way he moved his hands, made him seem older than he was.

"So interesting? Do tell." I was intrigued. His big-kid air amused me.

"My friends and I have been inspecting the part of the camp behind the sauna. Men who were covered in soot and smelled like smoke came from the other side of the fence. They went into the sauna and showered. We stayed outside and watched. They looked really sad and hung their heads. One of them ruffled my hair as he went by. His name's Leo. He isn't very old. I think he's only eighteen."

My son's story surprised me. I had heard that some other members of the camp used our showers, which were apparently some of the few in Birkenau with hot water.

"One of my friends asked them if they were bakers. The men gave a funny smile and said yes, and my friend told them the black bread they were baking tasted horrible. They laughed really hard at that and then the SS escorted them out toward those big houses at the back."

The story was more concerning than amusing to me. We all knew the rumors, but we tried not to think too much about it. Sometimes it was easier to avoid certain things. Like how some of the young women were forced into prostitution in exchange for food. The kapos picked out the girls who were all alone so the family would not get in the way. Virginity for Gypsies was extremely important.

I myself had been subjected to the handkerchief test at the party on the night before our wedding. Though I was not a Gypsy, I had to show my fiancé's family that I had not been with any man before Johann. It was embarrassing. My in-laws knew that I had loved Johann from early on.

MARIO ESCOBAR

Nothing and nobody had taken what I wanted to give my husband.

Once Otis fell asleep in my lap, Blaz started to tell me about his day. My oldest never ceased to amaze me. He was always looking out for the younger ones, and his ability to face the situation we were living in was astounding.

"The little ones don't know how to keep their mouths shut. It's better we don't know what goes on in those houses at the back," he began.

"That's true," I said.

"So is it true about the nursery school?" he asked.

"How do you know about that?" I pulled back, taken by surprise.

"People are already talking about it. You know there are no secrets here," he said seriously.

"What do you think of the idea?"

He was thoughtful for a few moments. Blaz was a deep thinker and did not like to answer without turning the matter over first.

His large dark eyes were starting to disappear in the darkness that spread throughout the barrack. "Do you really think they'll allow it?" he asked.

"They've asked me to run it," I answered.

"The Nazis never do something for nothing. I'll try to figure out what they're after."

His perspective surprised me. He had divined the spirit that moved the immense camp. Though we did not understand the inner workings of Auschwitz, we had figured out that everything had a reason; everything was geared toward some purpose. We were only a handful of cogs in the wheel of a much larger and more complex machine. My son was right about that: nothing happened without a definite purpose. Someone higher than Mengele had authorized him to open a nursery and school, so the doctor had to have supplied a convincing reason. In the middle of a war it was not easy to obtain all the supplies we were going to need.

"Don't go poking around trying to learn anything," I told him, fully aware that he would disobey.

"Don't worry. I'll help you any way I can. Do you know yet what ages will be there at the center?" he asked.

"It's all happening so fast; I haven't had time to plan anything yet. Tomorrow is going to be a really long day. We'd better sleep now."

"Yeah, I'm worn out," he answered, giving me a kiss.

"I love you, Blaz," I said while I pulled the blanket over him.

"I love you too, Mom." I could tell he was smiling.

I lay down and tried to sleep, but my mind kept turning everything over. That night I did not think about the husband I had not seen in weeks, or about what would become of our children, or about food. I could only think about the project. "A nursery school in Auschwitz," I said over and over to myself. Was it a cruel joke? Was it actually possible? I could perhaps save the camp's children, give them even a few hours' respite from the brutality all around us. It was worth a try. As a mother, I owed it not only to my own children but also to the rest of the little ones wandering around the camp half-naked, starving, with the haunted look of suffering.

E I G H T

MAY 1943
AUSCHWITZ

That morning I waited impatiently for Dr. Mengele to arrive. I had hardly slept a wink. When they called us for the morning count, I quickly got the children dressed and, after downing the abhorrent coffee, headed for the medical barrack. I did not typically arrive that early, but I did not want to lose any time. Anna had stayed with the baby we decided to call Ilse. None of us had been able to discover the child's real name. In a way, Ilse was the nursery school's first child, since now we were allowed to care for and protect the children.

Hearing the sound of a car's motor, I leaned over the rail. Ludwika showed up and came to stand beside me, her shoulder touching mine. *I've never wanted to see Dr. Mengele so much before*, I thought as a military car stopped beside the barrack. A light rain was falling, but I barely noticed it for the chill that ran up my spine.

Dr. Mengele walked through the mud with his firm, sure gait. His black boots shone and his uniform had recently been ironed. His hat was soaking wet, and the look of total indifference on his face made me tremble. He came up the few stairs that separated us, humming a tune under his breath. After glancing at us with palpable disdain, he nodded in greeting and went inside to change.

I did not dare detain him. Typically we had to wait for the SS to address us. A few minutes later, Mengele returned to the stairs in a white uniform holding a metal clipboard with a few blank pieces of paper.

"Frau Hannemann, would you be so kind as to come with me?" he asked, hardly looking my way.

We walked in silence to barrack 32. My heart was beating wildly, and I had to work hard to keep my breathing steady. He stepped back to let me pass, and I walked into the laboratory. Few of the medical staff had been allowed into Mengele's inner domain, only his direct assistants. The doctor was very jealous over his experiments and projects.

"I presume you have an answer for my proposal?" he said, tossing the clipboard onto the table before turning to look me straight in the eyes.

The doctor was not the typical blonde-haired, blue-eyed SS official. According to rumors, some of his colleagues called him "the Gypsy" because of his black hair and dark eyes.

"That's what I wanted to see you about," I said with a faltering voice. I was trying to order my words carefully, as if each syllable carried great weight. I was afraid he would have changed his mind.

"Then you . . ." he began, leaving the phrase incomplete.

"I would like to take on the responsibility of running the nursery school at Auschwitz, but I will need you to procure the necessary materials. I do not want it to be a place we just stick the children. I'm envisioning a space where the little ones can forget about the war and the losses they are having to face." My tone was resolute. I had managed to conquer my nerves.

"But of course. When I made the proposal, I was absolutely serious. You'll have everything you need. I want the children to be well cared for, for them to lack nothing. You can work with two or three assistants. A couple new nurses arrived a few days ago. I'll have them sent over tomorrow. The supplies will also begin arriving tomorrow," he said, smiling for the first time in our exchange.

He only smiled when he got his way. There was something both devious and infantile in his grin, but it meant that he was in a decent mood and that being in his presence held no imminent danger.

"Thank you," I managed to say.

"There's no need for thanks. I know most of you think we're all a bunch of monsters, and you may be right to a degree, but that's simplifying things greatly, don't you think? We're pursuing an ideal; we have a mission. It isn't easy to answer duty's call, but it is always gratifying. As long as I'm assigned here, those children will enjoy exquisite treatment, I assure you." The man could never help himself from preaching about duty and sacrifice.

Impatient with his rhetoric, I asked, "Where will the nursery and school be?"

"We've cleaned out barracks 27 and 29. They should be more than adequate," he answered.

That was more than what I was hoping for. The kindergarten could include a nursery for the younger ones and a little school for the older ones. Two barracks was an extremely generous offer. I quickly calculated how many children we could care for: nearly one hundred.

"You and your family will live in barrack 27. I think you'll be able to care for other people's children better if you don't have to worry about your own. I've learned that you have five children, including one set of twins," Mengele said.

For some reason I could not fully explain, his comment

made me nervous. My children were, to some degree, my weakness. The SS official knew that a mother would do anything for her children.

"Thank you, Herr Doktor."

"It's nothing. Now I need to get back to work. These are the keys to the barracks. I don't want the supplies getting robbed before we even start," he said.

When I went out, the air was heavy with smoke. When the wind was blowing toward camp, the air was barely breathable. Ludwika was waiting for me when I got to the medical barrack. Then we headed to the women's hospital quarters. She was impatient to know what had transpired but did not dare ask.

"We'll start tomorrow. They've given us barracks 27 and 29." As I spoke, I pointed to the buildings right in front of the hospital barracks.

"We can give you a hand. We're right next to you," Ludwika said.

We celebrated with a brief hug. Affectionate gestures were rare at camp. Then I went to see Dr. Senkteller. I had to tell him that starting the next day I would be leaving the hospital to run the nursery school.

"A nursery school. What a marvelous idea. My heart just sinks every time I see those children wallowing in the mud with nothing to eat," he said.

"Thank you. I hope I'm capable of running it in a place like this," I answered.

He rested his hand on my shoulder briefly and nodded. "Of course you're capable."

The morning dragged on forever. I was so eager to tell Anna and my children about the changes. After Dr. Mengele's most recent rounds of selections, the number of invalids in the hospital had dropped drastically. Most prisoners were now too afraid to go to the hospital, fearing that they would be sent away and never return.

That final afternoon of May, nearly four thousand more Gypsy prisoners arrived at the camp. The buildings filled up again, and the brief sense of balance from the last few weeks was lost. The resources were more or less the same for ten thousand prisoners as for fifteen thousand. The arrival of newcomers meant less food, less space, and more illnesses.

When the workday was finally over and I entered barrack 14, two hundred more people were now residing on the floors and in the few beds that had been empty.

Anna was with the baby, and my children were trying to kill time playing in front of the barrack. Some of the new children had joined them. It was easier for the younger ones to welcome the new arrivals than it was for the adults.

"New prisoners today," Anna said when she saw me, as

if it were not already obvious. She seemed overly tired, her body letting her know little by little that life was slipping away and that it desperately needed to rest. Anna had lived through some bright times, but most of her existence had consisted of interminable worry. I thought of how all her effort and striving had been in vain. If all of her children and grandchildren died, no memories of the old woman or her lineage would remain.

"I imagine they won't be the last," was all I could think to answer.

"We've only taken a few into our barrack, but the rest are bursting at the seams." She handed me the baby.

I asked, "Are there many new children?"

"Yes, from Bohemia, Poland, and all over. They've brought an entire orphanage that some Polish nuns were running," she said.

"How will we ever survive this?" I asked, discouraged. It seemed that just as things were starting to look less bleak, new complications arose.

"What happened with Dr. Mengele?" Anna was impatient for details.

"All good news. We'll open the nursery school. Tomorrow the supplies start arriving, as well as some women to help." My excitement started to return. "They've given us barracks 27 and 29."

Anna started telling all the women around us. Some danced for joy and others hugged me.

"How wonderful! Do you need help? We're free right now; we could go clean the barracks," Anna said.

I preferred to keep things well organized. If the SS saw fifty Gypsy women descending upon the barracks, they might complain to their management and our dream of having somewhere for the children would go up in smoke.

"No, I'll go over tomorrow with some women to get it all set up."

"Of course, you're right," Anna said, serious once again. "Forgive me. This poor old woman gets carried away sometimes."

"I will need your help, but at first I need to get things running smoothly," I said, caressing her cheek.

"There's even more good news. They've organized an orchestra in our camp. They're allowed to play certain days of the week. How we love to dance and sing!" The brightness had returned to her voice.

"That's wonderful!" I replied, smiling with her contagious euphoria. "Things are going to get better, little by little. Maybe a lot of the hardships we've been facing are just the result of how Birkenau was built so quickly, almost improvised. Things are going to get better." I needed to hear myself say it.

Still holding the baby, I made my way to my children. Blaz came up very excited. He was carrying a small violin, similar to the one Johann had given him a few years ago. Our oldest son did not have his father's gift, but he was still a very decent musician and could play quite well.

"Mom, I signed up for the band, and they accepted me. This morning I had my audition, and the director gave me the violin!" His eyes were dancing with excitement.

"Excellent, how truly excellent. It seems this day is bursting with good news," I said.

"You know, I'm going to miss this place," he said, waving his hand to indicate barrack 14. It was unbelievable how we could get used to this kind of life and even start to miss the misery and hardship.

"You can come back here whenever you'd like," I said.

Otis hugged me tightly, and as I passed my hands over his face I felt that his forehead was a little hot. One of my greatest fears was that my children would get sick. There was no medicine in the hospital, and invalids were not allowed to stay in bed longer than ten days. After that they were discharged, either back to the barrack or to leave in one of Dr. Mengele's selections.

We all went to bed after supper. It was one of our last nights in barrack 14, and we were all a bit unsettled. Not long ago, the people from this barrack had saved our lives.

I was profoundly grateful for everything they had done for us, but soon we would be living in the back part of the nursery school.

Since I had hardly slept at all the night before, it did not take me long to fall asleep. I dreamed of Johann. We were running through a forest in springtime on a carpet of flowers. My soul seemed intent on gifting me with sweet memories. Then we were on vacation during Holy Week, and my father had allowed us to go to the country by train. I spent the entire night before the trip fixing food, and I ran to the station at the first light of dawn so I would not lose a second of the adventure. Johann was already waiting for me with his customary smile. We held hands throughout the entire trip. Though I was aware of the looks of surprise on people's faces as they saw us, I was intent on capturing that unique, unrepeatable moment.

When we got to the charming little mountain town, we started out on the long, three-hour walk. My backpack weighed me down, but I enjoyed every step of the way. For a moment I imagined we were the first Adam and his wife, Eve, the only two humans on earth. No angry looks, no whispers as we walked by, no insults from Nazis who spit on Johann's shoes when they saw him holding hands with a German woman. We hiked up the narrow path, clambered up some steep crags, and suddenly an immense prairie opened up before us. It was one of the most beautiful places I had ever seen. We stretched a blanket under the shade of a tall pine tree and pulled out the food and a little sweet wine.

I do not know how long we spent there, but we got to the station at night. At the end of my dream, the beautiful prairie began to wither, the flowers wilted, and the gray skies threatened rain. That pristine garden slowly turned into a terrifying cemetery of the living dead. Barbed-wire fences sprouted and grew from the ground like weeds, and the water turned a stagnant, bloodred color. I awoke with a start. It was the first time I had had a pleasant dream since I had been in Auschwitz. Apparently my mind had started to relax. Yet the terrible ending reminded me again exactly where we were.

I decided that before going to the nursery school I would go see Elisabeth Guttenberger, the camp secretary. I wanted to know if anyone could tell me where my husband was, but I needed to figure out if I could trust her before asking for her help. Also, I needed to take her the list of everything we needed to get the nursery school up and running. Dr. Mengele had requested the basics, but we would need much more than that to do it well. Plus, they had to authorize the arrival of the two nurses who would be helping me, and I wanted to choose a Gypsy woman as my assistant. The children would feel much more comfortable with someone they already knew than with two nurses coming from a different section of Auschwitz.

I woke before most of the others and walked out in the cool, early June morning. The main road was still empty when I arrived at the offices. For the first time since I had arrived, the walk had seemed almost pleasant. My state of mind doubtless influenced this perception, as did the slowly warming temperatures and the slightly improved atmosphere of the Gypsy camp.

When I entered the office, Elisabeth was already at her post organizing files and lists of prisoners. The new Romani arrivals of recent days had increased the workload of all the internees. Germans tend to be very conscientious, keeping things well documented and organized. In that regard, the Gypsy camp was not much different from the bureaucracy that existed outside the electric fences.

"*Guten Morgen,*" I said, entering the office.

"*Guten Morgen,*" she replied with a smile.

"I didn't expect you to be so cheery. The number of prisoners has gone through the roof in the last few days," I said.

"Yes, but I also know why you're here. That there's going to be a nursery in the camp is very good news," she said.

"Rumors fly!" I smiled back.

"And when they're good rumors, we all recover a modicum of hope. The selections of the typhus patients were hard on everyone, besides all the unpleasantness that occurs on a daily basis around here. So good news is always welcome."

"This is a list of some of the supplies we'll need. Could you add it to what Dr. Mengele already turned in?" I asked, handing over my list.

Her eyebrows grew steadily higher as she studied my writing. Most of the things I had asked for had not been available since before the war. But she knew that if anyone could manage to get it, it would be the influential Dr. Mengele.

"The doctor has important contacts in Berlin. The director of the Kaiser Wilhelm Institute, von Verschuer, is his benefactor. He'll likely be able to send all this," Elisabeth said.

"I do hope so," I replied.

"The candidates to be interviewed are supposed to arrive in a few hours. Shall I send them directly to the nursery barracks?"

"Yes, please. I'd also like to include Zelma as one of my assistants," I requested.

"I'll send her right away to help you with cleaning out the barracks."

"I could also use two or three volunteer mothers."

"Very well. I'll send them all with cleaning supplies," Elisabeth said.

I left the office feeling that things were looking up for us in Auschwitz. I went straight to barracks 27 and 29. As I passed barrack 14, Blaz and Otis ran out to me. The younger three stayed with Anna so they would not get in the way of preparing the buildings. When I opened the wooden door of the first barrack, a rank odor of decay made us instinctively cover our mouths and noses. The boys hung back at the doorway until I went in first.

The barrack was poorly lit, as they all were. The only light came from a sort of skylight in the roof, though this barrack's original design had been modified to include two windows right beside each other and a larger window at the back. Yet wooden shutters covered the glass and only let in a faint glow of light. Blaz and Otis opened the windows and pushed the shutters apart. Light flooded the room, allowing me to really see the place. The main room was in slightly better condition than in our barrack. There was a wood floor over a semblance of a crawl space, which kept out some of the dampness and cold. There was a large iron stove in the middle of the room and a smaller one in the room at the back. There was no electricity or running water, but at least the children would have somewhere to go during the day.

"It's a pigsty," was Otis's evaluation.

"Well, it is for now, but in a few days it'll be so pretty you'll think you're back at school," I said, smiling.

"This is going to be a school?" Otis asked.

"Of course," Blaz answered with a slap on the back of Otis's neck. "The kids can come here and Mom will teach them."

"Oh, leave me be. The only thing I haven't missed is having to go to school," Otis complained.

"We'll have cartoon movies, notebooks, colored pens, and bread and milk. I think you'll like it," I said, trying to help him understand what this meant for the children at the camp.

"That's more like it," Otis said, smiling now. He licked his lips at the mere thought of bread and milk, already tasting the delicacies in his mind.

We each took one of the brooms I had brought and got to work sweeping. Clouds of dust billowed up at first, but the open windows slowly cleaned the air out. We found some scraps of rotten meat, rather unusual in our camp. We had not seen anything like that since we had arrived. After a few hours of scrubbing and disinfecting, we heard Zelma come in. She was a beautiful Gypsy with light-brown skin, green eyes, and pronounced Eastern facial features. She was very thin and had a green handkerchief covering her hair. Her faded, dirty dress could not hide her beauty. She had two young children who lived with her in barrack 16.

"Frau Hannemann, thank you for thinking of me for your assistant," the young woman said with her head lowered.

"Oh, please, don't call me Frau Hannemann; just call me Helene. I won't be your boss. I'll simply organize the school and nursery with your help."

"A real job at the camp always means life gets a little bit easier, and to get to take care of the children—this brings me such joy." Her eyes were bright as she spoke.

Surely Zelma had heard we would have bread, milk, and other things for the children. She knew that these "luxuries" might help her own survive.

I asked, "Do you think the other mothers will be willing to bring their children?" Some mothers were adamant about never being separated from their offspring, and understandably so. We heard rumors every day about children who were mistreated or who simply disappeared.

"If the children get real food, yes, I do. Most of our little ones are terribly thin. I've yet to see milk or real bread since we arrived."

We kept working all morning. At noon, Ludwika arrived with our lunch rations and the two Polish nurses Mengele had chosen to help us. The two Jewish women were very young and seemingly in good health, but they spoke no

German. The one named Maja was strawberry blonde with reddish cheeks and dark eyes; the other was Kasandra, a redhead with freckles and gray eyes. They seemed shy and rather scared, but that was to be expected. Judging by their appearance, they had not been at Auschwitz long, and the camp was intimidating, twisted enough to negate your will and your desire to live. I presumed that behind their bowed heads and sad eyes there were stories of persecution and pain. The selection was even more brutal for Jews than for Gypsies. Families were separated immediately upon arrival and, from what I had heard, camp conditions for Jewish men and women were even more pathetic than for us.

When the two Jewish nurses saw the canned green beans and peas that we were eating, they could barely keep themselves from jumping at the food. Ludwika served them a portion, and though the rations allowed us were hardly sufficient, it was at least more than the rest of the prisoners received.

"Eat slowly," Ludwika advised them in Polish.

I thought that the fact that they did not speak my language would be a problem, but we could not send them back to their camps. It would have been a death sentence for them. On the other hand, there were quite a number of Polish families in the Gypsy camp, and many children spoke only Polish.

After eating in silence, we continued preparing the first barrack and then moved on to the second. Our cleaning crew grew to include several Gypsy mothers who were free to help us in the afternoon, so the process went much quicker with the second barrack.

We finished right before time for the evening meal. It was still daylight, but the shadows were starting to stretch across the road. We walked back to barrack 14 tired but as content as was possible in that place. The next day the paint and other supplies would start arriving, and before long the school would be up and running.

For the first time since my arrival at Auschwitz, that night I felt the satisfied tiredness of having worked hard at a meaningful task. When we got to the doorway, the rest of the mothers gave us a hero's welcome.

The young Polish nurses had gone with Ludwika to sleep in the medical workers' barrack. I wondered how long it had been since they had slept between moderately clean sheets with a mattress under them.

Then we heard loud shouting from behind the barrack. Anna looked at me with her eyes popping in worry, and we all ran toward the commotion.

We saw a group of children huddled together at the barbed-wire fence. They were all crying and screaming. We pulled them apart. Anna was still holding baby Ilse, but she handed the child to me when she saw the limp body of her grandson tangled in the fence. Smoke rose from beneath his ragged clothing. Anna began shrieking and pulling out her hair in desperation.

The scene was horrific. We could not touch the child, who had surely been killed by the strong charge. For a few seconds I studied the horrified faces of my children. Emily, Ernest, and Adalia ran to me, their dirty cheeks streaked with tears. I thanked heaven they were safe, but my heart grew heavier as the moments passed. Anna would feel this deep hollowness in her heart the remainder of her days. Surely she had seen other loved ones pass away throughout her lifetime, but her young grandson had been one of the few joys she had left.

"Fremont!" she cried out in anguish. She tried to go closer to the child, but two mothers held her arms to stop her.

Two kapos and some guards came up. Without asking any questions, they immediately started hitting at the crowd with their nightsticks. It made no difference that there were pregnant mothers, children, and old women in our crowd. Most fled quickly, but Anna remained glued on her knees before the cadaver of the boy.

Irma Grese brought her bludgeon down heavily on Anna. Blood gushed from her forehead. Anna turned, caught my eyes for a split second. The children had run back to the barrack with everyone else, but I had stayed near my friend. The guards did not touch me; I bore the protective aura of Dr. Mengele.

"Leave her! Her grandson just died, and she can't even hold him!" I shouted, tears springing to my eyes.

"Shut your whore's mouth," Maria Mandel spit out at me.

The kapos tried to lift Anna and draw her away, but she flung them off and lunged to hold her grandchild. Immediately the fence lights flickered with the electric shock that was discharged. Anna jerked and contorted then fell to the ground, still clinging to the boy's body.

"Anna!" I screamed, trying to reach her, but the kapos held me back.

The two corpses lay there in an eternal embrace, united forever in love's victory over the infernal reality of Auschwitz. They were finally free. Nothing and no one could hold them back any longer. The kapos dragged me through the mud to the main road, and I fleetingly longed to share my friend's fate—to close my eyes and be forever free from life's fatigue and heartaches; to cut loose from the invisible threads that bound me to this world. Maybe it was better to throw myself against the fence and let my soul fly free from the tyranny of the body, rising above the Polish sky to a better place where humans no longer hurt one another.

Without Anna, I was alone again. Her sweet voice, her tiny eyes swimming in a sea of wrinkles, her pixie smile that captured her aged beauty: none of it existed any longer. Dust to dust and ashes to ashes. Death seemed like a gift from heaven, but I knew that it was not yet for me. I was an old ship in the middle of a storm, and my children anchored me to life. I had to keep fighting for them, trying to hold on to hope, looking each day in the face, praying for this nightmare to finally be over.

NINE

JUNE 1943
AUSCHWITZ

I had never seen Christmas come in June. Around ten o'clock in the morning, Dr. Mengele showed up in his convertible military car followed by four trucks. For once, their presence did not indicate a selection or a transfer. Instead, they were packed with school supplies, swings, toys, chairs, beds, and other items for the nursery and school. Everyone was up in arms. Half-dressed children ran after the trucks, many of the German kids singing a common school song as if they were trotting out to meet their teachers. The excitement spread among families who hitherto had experienced nothing but hardship, hunger, and death at the camp.

Dr. Mengele parked in front of barrack 27, a big smile

on his face. He stood and paused for a few seconds to study my team waiting at the bottom of the stairs and to look over the hundred-some-odd people, especially the children, patiently waiting for the supplies to be unloaded. He nonchalantly left the car and started fishing in his pockets. Then he handed a piece of candy to each of the children, smiling and tousling their hair.

When he was almost in front of me, he blew on a little whistle, and some twenty prisoners started unloading all sorts of articles from the trucks and taking them into the first building. Some of the things I recognized and indicated they should go in the next building.

"Frau Hannemann, I hope you're happy. I've managed to acquire everything you requested plus more. This will be the finest kindergarten in the region," the SS officer said with a verifiably childlike expression I had never observed in him before.

"Thank you very much, Herr Doktor. It's a fact that these children needed hope, and you have given it to them," I said, not drawing out my answer. It was never a good idea to speak at length with an SS officer in the presence of other Germans.

Irma Grese and Maria Mandel, the vicious female guards, flanked Dr. Mengele. Their severe frowns were a striking contrast to Mengele's affable expression. The scenes from last night were still burned onto my mind's eye, when they had commenced beating all the prisoners who had run to help the poor child electrocuted by the fence. They were very likely the last straw that made Anna decide to end her life. Did those women have no souls? I could not comprehend how they could resist a smile when seeing the joy of the children.

Grese met my gaze steadily. Her look held a bottomless hatred, as if she were disgusted by all that the doctor was doing for us. But then she started shooing people away and soon left with Mandel. The Nazis did not want large groups of people gathering together. They did, however, allow the children to remain in the vicinity.

One group of prisoners began putting together the swing set and the sandpit for the younger children. Another group started laying the wiring for electricity. We would not have running water, but Mengele had procured two large tanks that would help us store drinking water every day. This was a priceless luxury in a camp with infected, unsanitary water.

While the prisoners kept working, my team and I began painting the walls with bright colors and laying out the rugs decorated with animals. We wanted to hold the grand opening of both the nursery and the school the very next day. I took several colors of paint and a brush and went to work on a sign at the front of the barrack. The doctor was still outside the building supervising the progress of the men who, emaciated beneath their striped uniforms, tried to show no signs of weakness or exhaustion.

I painted each letter in a different color while Mengele looked on in silence. It was not his habit to spend so much time outside the hospital or the laboratory he had improvised in the sauna. I can only suppose he wanted to enjoy this moment.

From behind me, he asked, "Do you think everything will be ready by tomorrow?"

I did not bother to turn around for an immediate answer. I took my time finishing the g. Then, still holding the paint can in one hand and the brush in the other, I replied, "That's my hope. I want the children to get to use the place as soon as possible." I went on with the a.

"Excellent!" he exclaimed. "Tomorrow a commission from Berlin is arriving, and I wanted to show them what we are doing here."

Though I had presumed that the children's school was part of the Nazi propaganda machine, it seemed a bit early for them to showcase us to the world. One of the last times Johann and I had gone to the movie theater, before the movie they showed a short documentary on Theresienstadt, a camp in Bohemia where thousands of Jews had been deported yet were allowed to live an apparently normal life. The video showed bunk beds with curtains for privacy, nurses, people sitting at tables while reading, sewing, or chatting. Now I knew that it was all a lie, one of the Nazi-manipulated realities. In some way, the nursery at Auschwitz would play a hand in furthering the farce of a fake world in which the SS treated even their enemies well.

"What are you thinking about?" Mengele had come close and rested his hand lightly on my right shoulder. The gesture of proximity shook me. I preferred to see the Nazis as inhuman monsters. The more human they acted, the more horrifying they became, as it meant any and all of us were capable of becoming as despicable as they were. Evil was given free rein between the fences of that ghastly nightmare.

"Everything will be ready," I managed to say at last. I wanted to end the conversation and think no more about how the Nazis managed to use us all and turn us into what we despised.

"Wonderful! Excellent work, Frau Hannemann!" the doctor exclaimed. He removed his hat and quickly ran his fingers through his dark hair, parted on the side.

I heard boots walking away on the strips of wood. I turned and watched him saunter down the main road, children swarming behind him. No one had told them that man was their jailer. Now the children were fond of him, and he knew how to draw out their smiles and affection.

I finished the sign and studied it for a moment. Then a very different voice behind me asked, "Is the doctor a good guy or a bad guy, Mom?"

I turned to find Otis, who was already outgrowing his clothes. His lower legs were bare, covered in bruises and scratches. In that, at least, he was like most other children still living free on the other side of the barbed-wire fence. I did not know how to answer his question. There was no doubt that Mengele was a criminal like everyone who held us at Auschwitz against our will. He may have acted nicer than some of the soldiers or guards, but that did not change the fact that he was one more executioner. I hesitated in my answer because I needed to warn my son not to get too close to the doctor without having him run around telling everyone in the camp that I was speaking out against Mengele.

"The people who are keeping us locked up here are not our friends. I don't want you to hate them, but keep your distance. Does that make sense?" I kept it short and simple.

Otis went back to playing his games, and then Blaz came up with a bucket of paint and said quietly, "The soldiers pay some of the girls to sleep with them. Some of the kapos and one of the old men organize it all. A teenager named Otto told me; he has to clean up their rooms afterward. Some of the girls are forced to go, and others volunteer in exchange for food."

I was horrified that my son knew all of this. He was having to grow up very quickly and was not ready to understand the crude realities of life.

"Stay away from them!" The anger rang out in my words. I was afraid these people would destroy more than the bodies of my children.

Kasandra and Maja came out of the barrack, saw my angry expression, and then hurried back inside, their heads lowered.

"I'm sorry, sweetie, but I just don't want anything to happen to you. From here on out I don't want you going too far from the nursery barracks. Do you understand?"

Now Blaz lowered his head. "Yes, Mother."

When I went back inside the barrack and saw how everything was coming along, I started to calm down. The colorful walls made the place special, a kind of oasis in this desolate desert in the middle of Poland.

Zelma's eyes were glowing. "It's just lovely!" she said. She was so encouraged that I tried to perk up. After all, the place was a ray of hope in the midst of the darkness.

After several hours of preparing our area, I called everyone together to eat and talk about how to organize the work. Taking care of dozens of children would not be easy. We needed to be prepared and well organized. After we ate, Ludwika stopped in and helped translate for the two Polish nurses who understood hardly any German.

"We need to let mothers know that the nursery and school will be open tomorrow. We don't know how many children are here at the camp. It could be up to a hundred. A few days ago they brought at least forty from the orphanage in Stuttgart. Not all of them are young, but a good number are," I said, putting some folders in order.

Maja asked, "What hours will we be open?"

"I think it's reasonable to go from 8 a.m. to 2 p.m.," I answered.

The other Jewish nurse, Kasandra, said, "But it's too many children for the number of caretakers."

"You're right." I nodded. This had also concerned me. The youngest children would need constant supervision, especially the babies.

"What if we ask three more mothers to help us? They could be Gypsy mothers who know other languages spoken here at the camp," Ludwika suggested. From the start, she had wanted to be involved in the center's activities.

I jotted down everything we were talking about to be able to run all the details by Mengele. We needed his approval for the center to work well.

"Do you think it will be hard to convince the mothers to leave their children with us?" I asked Zelma, still worried about that thought.

"Some Gypsy mothers, myself included, are very jealous over their children. But I think we all realize that our kids will receive things here that they can't get in the barracks. Most of the children are wasting away."

"You're right. Our mission this afternoon is to tell all the mothers at the camp. And the adults looking after orphans," I said.

"Don't you feel a bit rushed to open tomorrow?" Ludwika asked, puzzled by my haste.

"Well," I said, sighing, "it seems that visitors are coming to the camp tomorrow, and Dr. Mengele wants the children's center to be in full swing."

Ludwika shook her head. It was not the first time the Nazis had organized a guided tour for the higher-ups from Berlin. It made us feel like animals in a zoo, on display for the enjoyment and mockery of our executioners. I tried to change the subject and encourage my team.

"We've got school supplies, little smocks, tables, chairs, two chalkboards, chalk, trash cans; the stoves are working, even though we don't need them right now. The movie projector is working, and we have five animated films. They've put in electricity and, most important of all, we have food!

Milk, bread, some vegetables, some sausages, and some nonperishables like powdered milk, cans of meat and fish, baby food, and basic medicines for fevers or common infections." I could not help smiling.

The women burst out in applause at the joy of that day. Such effusive demonstrations of contentment were so rare that we all looked around to see if anyone had heard us. The only ones who came up at the sound of our celebration were my children. They had been playing in the small room we had outfitted for us to live in.

Adalia came out with a milk mustache above her smiling mouth. For the first time since we had arrived, she looked fully awake and aware. Our poor nutrition had weakened the children's bodies and dampened their spirits, but they perked up quickly with real food in their stomachs. The twins were playing with some of the new toys, and the older two were holding notebooks and pencils.

"Go back to playing. Nothing's wrong," I said. They all smiled and went back to our new room.

"They look so good!" Ludwika exclaimed.

"Yes, thank God." I could not help smiling with relief. I no longer felt completely like a prisoner. The fences had grown almost transparent to my eyes. My soul itself felt free. Those violent murderers could never own it. I knew that happiness for us was, to a large degree, unhappiness for them. They ate better than we did, went out on the weekends, and slept with whomever they wanted to. They themselves were hardly more than ruthless animals or heartless children playing with us as with broken toys, except that their wanton choices meant life or death for hundreds of people.

We continued to work awhile longer and then went out in pairs to talk with the camp's mothers. We had to convince them all to have their children dressed and ready by eight o'clock the next morning. The four Gypsy mothers would walk by each barrack to collect the children.

As I walked with Zelma, she brought up the subject of Anna.

"Anna would have been glad to know what we're doing right now."

"Yes, but she's in a better place now. It seems like dying is the only way to leave Auschwitz."

"I know a couple of Gypsies who managed to escape. They were in the group that built this camp, but now the security is much tighter."

We walked nearly to the end of the camp toward the bathrooms. It was the free hour, and we figured several mothers would be washing their children. As we passed the last barrack I caught sight of one of the trains. A huge crowd was scrambling to grab hold of their belongings while the selection took place. I had nearly forgotten that a few weeks ago I had arrived on one of those horrible transport cars. I thought again of Johann, of how I still knew nothing about him after all this time. I had to find time tomorrow to ask Elisabeth Guttenberger.

"What's on your mind? You're rather quiet all of a sudden," Zelma said.

"I was thinking about our hellish trip from Berlin," I answered.

"I came from the Lodz ghetto. For some reason all the Gypsies were to be sent here. I'd been in that hellhole since 1941, and that's where my daughter was born. My son had already been born. It was extremely difficult to find food, and the Jews discriminated against us, which made it even harder to find work. The only people making any money at all in the ghetto worked in the industries in the surrounding areas. Finally, my husband managed to get a job in a tire factory, and things weren't quite as abysmal." Zelma's eyes were half-closed and her voice low as she spoke through the painful recollections.

"What happened to your husband?" The words were out of my mouth before I could stop them. The question would only upset her more. She merely hung her head.

We watched the unfortunate travelers who had arrived at their life's final destination. These cars had brought well-dressed individuals, surely from some wealthy city in Bohemia or Poland. But their kempt appearance would not last long. Within a few days they would struggle to recognize themselves in a mirror. Yet at that moment many of them were still arrogant and demanding, as if they were mere tourists making a stop at the Birkenau spa and resort or a ski lodge in the Alps.

The Germans were remarkably subdued, attempting to calm the passengers without the use of force. For some reason, a little blonde girl caught my eye. She seemed lost in the crowd. She was wearing a pretty green coat and held a cute little suitcase in her hand. The poor thing was crying and walking back and forth trying to find her family. An officer holding another little girl's hand came up to her. The two girls were exactly alike, like two drops of water. The officer knelt down and started stroking the girls' heads. From where we were, we could not tell who it was, but when he stood up, I knew without a doubt that it was Mengele.

The officer put one of his assistants in charge of the twins and then took his place in front of the large groups the recent arrivals had been divided into. He commenced gesturing with his hand to the right or the left. I could not make out his facial expression from where I stood, but his body seemed calm and relaxed, like he was doing an ordinary daily task. I remembered how an officer like

Dr. Mengele had separated my husband from the rest of us. Anger and rage started churning in my stomach, and I thought I might vomit.

Zelma noticed me growing pale. "Are you okay, Frau Hannemann?" she asked.

"Yes, just a little dizzy," I choked out, doubling over. At that moment a fit of heaving overtook me, and I could not hold back. I vomited right there on the muddy ground of the road. I felt like my stomach was going to fly out my mouth. Somehow my spirit had understood that I was serving the devil himself, though I had tried to deny it with my mind.

We went back to the nursery barracks. My children were impatient to eat and go to bed. They all wanted tomorrow to hurry up and come so they could see the nursery school's inauguration with their own eyes. I tried to go along with it, but I had lost all the excitement I had once felt. I envisioned the visit with the Nazi hierarchy the next day and felt like vomiting again.

Zelma said good-bye at the door and promised to be back tomorrow with the other three helpers. I trusted her. Despite being very young, she was a valuable companion. Besides, I could relate to her. We had both lost our husbands, though I still clung to the hope of seeing mine again.

There were two beds in our room. Blaz would sleep

with Otis and the twins in one, and Adalia and I would take the smaller bed. Compared to the damp, wretched pallets of the barracks, our new situation seemed like a luxury hotel. The workers had insulated the walls and roof well. It felt clean, dry, and warm.

Before the little ones went to sleep, we read one of the new stories. It had been so long since we had seen a book. The three younger children were mesmerized as I slowly turned the pages full of pretty pictures. By the time I finished, Adalia was asleep. I tucked her in and then carried the twins to the other bed.

"Good night, my angels," I said, very aware that it was the first time we had been alone all together since we had arrived at the camp.

One of the many things Auschwitz stole from its prisoners was the right to individuality and privacy. We were never alone. We could hardly think or reflect. When hunger was not tormenting you, pain, terror, and humiliation turned your mind into an automaton.

"Mom, could you sing us the song?" Emily asked. Her lovely clear eyes looked into mine so intently.

"Of course, but only once tonight."

My voice sounded so strange as it broke the silence of the barrack. I could hardly recall what I sounded like when singing, but soon enough the song called up memories from my childhood and happier times with my own children. They were all special to me. They were the strong links in the chain that anchored my life. From Blaz, the oldest, to Adalia, the youngest, they were each absolutely unique and unrepeatable. They had their own personalities, preferences, and opinions. I loved them with my entire being. The fact that we were all alive by that point in the war was nothing short of a miracle. I trembled as the last few lines of the lullaby came out of my mouth. In some ways I felt like I had felt that morning at the top of the stairs outside our apartment, when I had hoped so desperately that misfortune would once again pass me by; but this time I was the one chosen to become part of the giant web of terror that was the system of German concentration camps.

The last few words of the lullaby escaped my mouth in a sad, melancholic tone. Yet children's lullabies are always hushed, to soothe little ones to sleep. When I glanced at the twins again, they had succumbed to sleep. Blaz and Otis kissed my cheek good night and lay down next to each other.

Before turning in myself, I put a sweater on and went out to the main room. I turned the light on and just looked at everything for a few seconds: the pictures on the walls, the school tables, the chalkboard. I felt like I was moving in a dream. This was the Auschwitz kindergarten—it sounded preposterous, but it was real. The next thought that crossed my mind was to wonder where the Nazis had found all these supplies. I knew I should not ask such questions, but I could not help but think that all these wonderful things had belonged to some nearby school that the SS had dismantled to build our own.

I sat at one of the little desks and took out a notebook with graph paper. I chose a pen and started writing:

Dear Johann:

I know that it's ridiculous for me to tell you about my life here at the camp. Surely you're somewhere just as bad or worse than here, but we always used to talk about everything, didn't we? When you lost your job and I was nine months pregnant with Adalia, while the kids were at school, we would walk for hours through Berlin's streets. They no longer let social pariahs like us into the parks, but the beautiful boulevards of the city were enough to keep us dreaming. We talked about going to America and how life would be when Germany woke up and turned its back on Hitler, but mainly we discussed all the little details of the children and the stories from the week.

I needed to spill out my feelings and fears on that school paper.

I feel that same way now, like this notebook lets
me take a long walk with you. You're not by my side
anymore, but we're still walking together, arm in arm,
staring destiny right in the face . . .

Writing a diary in my current situation felt like a way
to mock the brutal oppression of our executioners. They
wanted to steal everything, including our memories.
My cramped writing built a protective fence around the
memories so nobody would dare try to rob them. Maybe
it was my way of exorcising the danger that constantly
floated above our heads. There was an ever-present death
sentence that had all our names written on it. Sooner or
later, we all have to die, but in the concentration camp it
felt like you did not actually die; you merely ceased to exist.
Entire families were snatched up, and few ventured beyond
the electric fences alive ever again. No one would remember them; their memory would dissipate like fog under the
burning sun. Smoke, an infinite nothing, a nonexistent void
in which the self becomes a mere sigh exhaled into eternity.
I believed we were immortal. My parents had always told
me our names were in God's memory for all time. But the
Nazis wanted to erase us from the face of the earth and
leave us forever in the limbo of the unborn.

TEN

JUNE 1943
AUSCHWITZ

I woke earlier than usual to get ready for the first day of class. In a few hours Dr. Mengele would be arriving with some Nazi bigwigs, and I wanted them to have a good impression of the nursery and the school. We had barely had any time to get organized, and this was a new endeavor for all of the workers. My children slept on while I laid out the school supplies and set up a film on the projector. Then I went to the other barrack to see how things were going. When I opened the door, I saw Maja and Kasandra. They were young but so eager to do their best. We smiled at one another, and they tried to greet me in German. While we finished getting things in order, I grew more and more anxious wondering if Zelma had managed to find three other helpers and if they had convinced the Gypsy mothers to trust their children to us for half the day.

I went back to the nursery barrack and saw a group of children coming down the road. They were the orphans who had arrived a few days ago, and the Nazis had housed them in barrack 16. Only the youngest of the orphans were in the group, and they were in a deplorable state. They were dirty, their hair greasy and full of lice. A young man who had been put in charge of taking care of them—and who was evidently not doing a very good job—had brought them.

"The children can't come to the nursery and school like this. We'll take them to the sauna to cut their hair and shower first," I said, frowning at their caretaker.

Maja and Kasandra came to help me. I took one of the littlest ones by the hand, and my anger slowly turned to pity. These poor wretches had lost their parents. After living in an orphanage run by nuns, they had been dumped in this awful place by the Nazis. I helped the youngest ones get undressed. Their skinny, fragile bodies were covered in dirt, bruises, and sores.

"Thank you. You're doing it just like my mother used to," one little brown-haired girl told me as I scrubbed her in the hot water. That broke my heart. I could easily be the mother of all these lost creatures.

I had to swallow hard to keep the tears back. How

much suffering had come from this war and, above all, from the evil of those who believed they were superior because of the color of their skin, their background, or their language. When we finished washing the children, we put clean clothes on them and led them back to the barracks. Another group had arrived. Most of them were twins, many of whom were not Gypsies. A few days ago Mengele had started bringing them from the selections and kept them under the care of a woman in barrack 32, where his personal laboratory was. We all wondered why, but few of us asked out loud. The rumors about his experiments had spread throughout the camp. We knew that he was in Auschwitz for reasons very different than caring for poor Gypsy prisoners. I could not deny that his interest in twins made me nervous. I did not want him getting near my children, and I forbade them from going anywhere near his laboratory.

We divided the children up by ages. We had over fifty little ones between three and seven years of age, and not all the camp's children had arrived yet. When the poor things went into the nursery and school barracks and saw the painted walls, desks, pencils, and notebooks, they reacted either with speechless staring or with excited cries. Most of them had not seen a formal school in years, and for many it was their first time to set foot inside a classroom. While the two Polish nurses tended to the older children, I got the younger ones settled in the nursery. When finally they were all seated with their school smocks on, I started serving breakfast. My three younger children were at one of the tables. Otis had gone to the other barrack, but Blaz had decided to stay to help me with the nursery. At eleven years of age, he would no longer be a student, but now he could help as my assistant.

Despite their hunger, all the children waited patiently for their cups of milk. Then we passed out biscuits. Stale as they were, they tasted like freshly baked cake to the young prisoners.

Zelma showed up a bit late, but she had managed to bring almost all the remaining children in the camp. Two Gypsy mothers went with part of the group to the other building, while one stayed with Zelma to help me.

We sat the children at the tables that remained, and they had breakfast like the others. When they had finished eating, we started a file for each child. It was nearly noon by the time we were finished. There were seven nationalities represented in the room of Jewish and Gypsy children. It would not be easy to integrate them all. We would teach them in German and Polish, which were the most common languages spoken among them.

We brought the children from both buildings together

and showed a Mickey Mouse film. Everyone knew Adolf Hitler loved Disney cartoons and that, before the war, Walt Disney himself had been associated with the Nazis. Unfortunately, many of Hitler's ideas had made their way to the United States and the United Kingdom. But none of that mattered to the children. Most of them had never seen a cartoon. They were hypnotized by the mouse hopping and running around with his dog Pluto. We used the film as break time outside for the adults, leaving Blaz to keep an eye on the children.

The Polish nurses shared a cigarette while the Gypsy mothers sat on the stairs and had some bread and cheese. Zelma stayed beside me. I looked to the other side of the barbed-wire fence. The yard around the hospital was bigger than the other yards, and the open space was sometimes used for soccer games between the *Sonderkommandos* and the Nazi guards. The previous Sunday we had all lined up near the fence to watch a game. The games and the concerts from our Gypsy band were the only forms of entertainment we were allowed in the camp.

"Are you pleased?" Zelma asked. "Everything has gone just like we planned."

"Yes, I am, though I wish we could get the Nazi visit over with," I said, a bit preoccupied. I knew that any passing comment or the slightest whim of the German hierarchy would carry great weight with the camp commando. We could not afford the slightest slipup.

"It'll be fine," Zelma reassured me, her deep eyes turned fully on me. "The barracks are adorable, and the children really seem different—happier and healthy."

"You're more of the optimist than I. They've only spent one day with us," I answered with a smile. I appreciated Zelma's outlook. Optimism was hard to come by in Auschwitz.

I heard the roar of several motors and looked up the road to see four dark vehicles advancing slowly through the Gypsy camp. I got so nervous I started giving orders like a madwoman. I straightened the aprons of all our helpers and told them to act natural and pretend not to be nervous, even though I was clearly frenetic.

When the procession came to a stop some sixty feet from the children's school, I went down the steps and had the helpers all line up in an orderly fashion like we were a group of soldiers about to be inspected. I did not even want to watch. I simply stood stock-still in front of the other women.

I did not see him come up, but when I heard a voice and lifted my head, there before me was Heinrich Himmler himself, the *Reichsführer-SS*. I recognized him from the newsreels that ran before the movies in the theaters. I had never attended a Nazi rally before, and I had refused to allow my children to participate in the Hitler Youth, though they would not have been allowed anyhow because of their father's race. Himmler did have a powerful presence. His pale face and little eyes behind round glasses gave him the look of a common government worker. But we all knew he was among the most powerful men of the Third Reich. His voice was soft and his dress impeccable, as if he were above all the misery that surrounded him and which he himself had created.

He smiled at me and said kindly, "Are you the school's director? Herr Doktor Mengele has spoken very highly of you. A German is just what's needed in a place like this."

I could not think of what to say. I was trembling slightly as I stared dumbly at him. It was like I was a little girl again, facing a strict teacher. Finally, I stuttered out, "Thank you, *Reichsführer-SS*."

"Is this the nursery?" Then, turning to the rest of his party, he said, "How can the Communist and Jewish trash call us inhumane?" They all laughed.

The *Reichsführer-SS* nodded in greeting to the rest of my helpers but did not extend his hand to them. Perhaps he feared contamination from the lower races. Dr. Mengele, all smiles, came forward and introduced me to the camp commandant, Rudolf Höss.

MARIO ESCOBAR

"Very nice work, Frau Hannemann. Dr. Mengele has mentioned your skill and dedication. Germans always appreciate the opportunity to show what we're made of," he said, lifting his eyes to the sign I had painted the day before.

Mengele just kept smiling and then, with his hand on my back, directed me to show the facilities to the visitors. The three men and the rest of the party stepped back for me to pass through, and when I went into the barrack I asked the children to stand up. Blaz turned the projector off, and the women quickly opened the wooden shutters to let the soft light of the Polish spring filter through the windows.

The children looked at the men with fearful eyes. The SS uniforms demanded respect from all prisoners. Even the youngest children knew it was better to stay away from anyone wearing a uniform with a swastika. The only one they did not seem to fear was Mengele, who knelt down before the children at the first table and handed out candies.

"This place has no reason to be jealous of most other German schools," Himmler said, his hands on his waist.

Höss replied, "We want the Gypsy children and Herr Doktor's twins to live in the best conditions possible."

"Thank you, Commandant," Mengele said with a slight bow of the head.

Himmler turned to me. "How many children are in the kindergarten?"

"We have a total of ninety-eight children. Fifty-five are here in the nursery and the other forty-three are in the school," I replied.

"In what language is the instruction given?" he asked.

I was a bit unsure how to respond. "In German and Polish." I was afraid he would be displeased that we taught in Polish.

But he only rubbed his chin and said, "Excellent."

Himmler knelt down close to one of the children. It was a Gypsy boy named Andrew who, with no trace of fear, stared right back into the commandant's eyes. The Nazi took off his hat and ran his fingers through his hair before asking the boy, "Do you like school?"

"Yes, Herr Commandant," the child answered very seriously. He was barely four years old, but he seemed quicker and more alert than most children his age.

"Have you had a good breakfast?" the officer asked.

"Yes, we've had milk and biscuits," Andrew said.

"Just what I had when I was a boy." The German smiled. Then he lifted his eyes and looked at the rest of the class. Before standing up, he spoke to another boy and said, "Do you know what those big chimneys on the other side of the fence are for?"

The boy was quiet for a moment, thinking. Then with mischief in his eyes, he answered, "That's where they bake the bread for the camp. The bakers make bread for us every day."

The answer pleased Himmler, who stood, ruffled the boy's hair, and said good-bye to the class. The children answered him in chorus. All the officers filed out of the room, and I followed.

"Everything is in order," the camp commandant said, "but I think you should spruce the children up a bit more. I know that Gypsies have an unpleasant odor naturally, but you really must do something about the horrible smell."

His comment made my insides boil. He knew perfectly well that my own children were Gypsies, but to these men we were little more than animals, though I was sure they treated their dogs better than us. I tried to soften my face and voice.

"Yes, Herr Commandant."

The last one to bid me farewell was Dr. Mengele, who squeezed my shoulders with his cold, bony hands. Smiling, he said, "Good work. We'll talk later."

When the party of visitors returned to their cars and drove out of the Gypsy camp, we all breathed easier. While my assistants gave the children something to eat before it was time to take them back to their barracks, Ludwika came to see me. She seemed rather worked up, though the hospital barrack had been spared the visit from the Nazi officials, who were too concerned with contracting something.

"How did things go?" she asked.

"Very well, I think. Though with the crows in black, one never knows," I said, making light of it. I needed to relax.

"Let's go for a walk," my friend suggested.

We walked away from the barracks toward the back of the camp. In the huge station where the trains stopped—it just so happened that there were none that morning—several members of the Auschwitz women's orchestra had set up. When the cars of Himmler's party approached, they started playing. Alma Rosé, an Austrian violinist in charge of the women's orchestra, was directing the group. Perhaps their minds escaped the barbed-wire fences as they played, but, like caged birds with broken wings, their music was melancholic.

Ludwika sighed as the cars paused briefly in front of the female prisoners. As always, the sound of the violin made me think of Johann, wherever he might be right then. I feared the worst had happened to him, but every night I begged God to protect him and to reunite us. I imagined the Creator of the universe had a great deal of work to do that summer of 1943, but most humans feel that their personal problems are the biggest on earth.

"Do you think we'll ever get out of here alive?" Ludwika asked as the band played on.

I studied the blue sky, then the woods beyond us that

were turning a dark green and the flowers that were timidly peeking up through the grass. Spring and summer had managed to come despite the bombs and the cadavers scattered over half a world of fields. The seasons were the strongest proof that life would continue once all this was over.

"We'll get out of here, though I'm not sure if it'll be alive or dead. They can only keep our bodies locked up, this mess of bones and flesh that slowly turns to dust, but never our souls."

I was shocked to hear the words coming out of my mouth. I did not usually talk about death at the camp, much less with a friend, but there was something liberating about knowing that the Nazis were incapable of exterminating my soul.

In silence we went back to the barracks, and the hullabaloo of the children revived our spirits. The students filed out in orderly fashion and separated into three groups. The first headed toward the orphanage barrack, the second to the barrack Mengele had outfitted beside his laboratory, and the third returned to their families throughout the camp.

Maja and Kasandra helped me tidy up the rooms, and then I ate with my children. I was very tired. The stress of the day had exhausted me. I wanted the children to go to bed early so I could write a few pages in my journal and then go to sleep myself. Sleep offered one of the few opportunities for us to feel truly free.

The children ate with big smiles on their faces. They no longer had to go to the infectious camp bathrooms, they were eating better, and our simple room seemed like a palace compared to barrack 14.

After reading a story to the younger ones and kissing the older ones, I closed the door and sat down in one of the small chairs. Hardly two minutes later I heard one of the children walking around and turned to find Blaz. The candle I had lit barely illuminated his dark features, but I did not need to see his face to know he wanted to tell me a secret.

"Are you all right, honey?" I asked, gesturing for him to come closer. He sat on my lap as if he were a much younger boy and let me cuddle him a few moments.

Blaz had been the first to invade our peaceful rhythm as a couple. He was like his father in so many ways, though with my persistence and obsession for order.

"When they took our IDs and everything we'd brought with us, I managed to keep something in my clothes. I haven't wanted to tell you 'til now. I was afraid you'd be mad. Every night I hold it and occasionally pull it out to look at it."

"What in the world is it? You've got me on the edge of my seat," I said, impatient.

He said nothing but pulled out a small photo and held it out to me. We were all there. I was pregnant with Adalia. We had taken the picture the summer before Johann had been removed from the orchestra. The war had not yet begun, and though we were starting to have some problems with the Nazis, life was still pretty peaceful and happy. I stared for a long time at our smiling faces. The image had captured a moment of joy and made it eternal. We were no longer that happy family posing in a park in Berlin. The summer air, the sound of the band in the background, the smell of cotton candy—it all seemed as far away as my childhood. Yet the picture held us in it forever.

I began weeping, and Blaz clung to me. I felt his arms around me, his cheek rubbing against mine. Our tears mingled, as once our blood had done when he was in the womb. For a few seconds, we were once again one body, joined by the umbilical cord. I closed my eyes and called up Johann's face. I wished with every fiber of my being that he were there with us. A family together again. As happy as in that moment lost in the memory of a black-and-white photo.

"Thank you, sweetie," I said between sobs.

He pulled away enough to look at me with his teary eyes. Blaz did not cry often. He had always been a strong, determined child.

"I'll take care of you, Mom. I'll take care of everyone until Dad gets back," he spluttered. "I know he's somewhere nearby. I can feel it. I miss lying next to him during our afternoon naps, playing violin together at the living room window, walking beside him and dreaming about being big like him someday."

"You will be, my little *Knirps*," I said and pulled him back into my arms.

Our breathing settled into a rhythm while the room cooled down with a northern breeze. The glaring Auschwitz floodlights penetrated the windows, blocking out the stars and moon. Someday, when that camp was dark and silent, the celestial orbs would again bathe it in their pure light, as they had always done, and the world would once more be a good place to live.

ELEVEN

AUGUST 1943
AUSCHWITZ

Exhaustion is time's best friend. It lets us turn the pages quickly, like in a bad book. Sometimes it's a mix of anxiety to know how the story ends and the apathy that results from the daily grind, even though this is the horrible daily grind of Auschwitz. It's been several weeks since I've poured out my heart on these pages, but in a way that's normal. Nothing noteworthy has happened until today. The days have gone by with neither rest nor any big news. That nothing ever happens is a good sign in the camp. Because in Auschwitz, when something happens, there are always bad consequences.

The arrival of new victims to this inhumane machine of destruction ends up affecting the entire camp and the moods of our guards.

Since summer started, many more people have come to the camp. Most of them seem like fish jerked out of the water, trying to breathe in hot air that kills them slowly. I don't know what it's like in the rest of Birkenau, but in the Gypsy camp, overcrowding is a serious problem, and we're all afraid of another typhus epidemic and having to go through the disinfection routines we barely survived in the spring. The infernal heat, the constant thirst, and the scarcity of food make us all vulnerable to disease, and I'm scared for my children. Dear Johann, how I long to see you and rest in your strong, safe arms.

Dr. Mengele has been on edge the past few weeks, but he's always kept his word about supplying us with food and school materials. He's proud of the nursery school and never stops praising my work, but I'm very uncomfortable if we're ever alone together. It's not that he's impolite, quite the opposite. Maybe it's his cold stare. It seems to come from an infinite emptiness.

"Mom!" Ernest called, rubbing his eyes. I was deeply wrapped up in the journal, and his cry jerked me out of it abruptly. In many ways, writing allowed me to live another life.

It was the birthday of the twins, the first celebration we would have since we had arrived at the camp. A few months ago I never would have dreamed of having a party here, but our situation had improved notably.

"Why are you up so early? Come here," I said, holding out my arms to him.

The twins were always together, as if two people living one life, but occasionally Ernest liked to be alone with me.

"It's our birthday. Did you forget?" he asked. His voice was still raspy from sleep.

"How could I forget? Seven years ago my belly stretched from here to the wall and I was sweating like a pig. I was trying to have a baby, but God gave me two!" I snuggled him close.

I caught sight of my bony arms. Since we had arrived at the camp, I had lost at least thirty pounds. I had still been carrying a slight pudge from my last pregnancy, which Johann loved, but even so I had been slim and muscular before the drastic weight loss at Auschwitz.

Emily showed up with her light-brown mane of hair. She looked so much like her brother, but her feminine features and long hair made them seem more different than they actually were.

She hugged me from the other side, and the three of us remained like that for a while, in silence, as the morning made its arrival within the wire fencing.

Time had snuck up on me, and I had to hurry to get the children ready before the students arrived. The camp's mothers had grown accustomed to sending their children to the nursery and school. They knew the children were well cared for and that they would get more food than if they stayed in the barracks. There were rumors that Dr. Mengele mistreated them, but I had never seen him do anything even slightly inappropriate to a child. Many of the children got sick and died, but that was normal for the camp. The water was unsanitary, the food insufficient, our clothing threadbare, and most of the children were locked up in barracks that would swelter in the summer and freeze in the winter.

Half an hour later, the barracks were overrun with children. We were already beyond our capacity, and the rations of milk and bread did not go as far, but it was still better than the food available in the rest of the camp.

The teachers began their classes, and I focused on my morning routine. I spent the first part of the day visiting our children who had gotten sick, most of whom were housed in the hospital in front of our barracks, checking in with Ludwika, visiting the children who had not come to school that day to see if I could help their mothers with anything, and then taking the list of supplies needed in the nursery school to Elisabeth, the Gypsy camp secretary.

As I walked up the main road toward the camp entrance, I always thought about the same thing: the hope that Elisabeth might have some news about my husband's whereabouts. She had been helping me try to find him for over two months, but Auschwitz was a gigantic monster that housed tens of thousands of people, and every day more joined the ranks of famished prisoners that comprised our impossible society.

As I drew near the camp entryway, I always prayed not to come across Irma Grese or Maria Mandel. That day I was lucky and got to the office without running into anyone. As soon as I entered, Elisabeth greeted me with a smile. She was an expressive young woman, but she did not typically grin when she greeted me.

"Good morning, Elisabeth," I said, returning the smile.

"Frau Hannemann, I believe it is the twins' birthday; do wish them happy birthday for me."

"Why don't you come by later on for the little party we're going to have?" I asked. Office staff did not typically wander down into the camp, but it was not forbidden.

"I might just do that. Did you bring a list for me?" She stretched out her hand.

"Yes, it's long today. More and more children just keep coming," I offered by way of explanation.

She looked the paper over carefully and then, with a wide smile, said, "And I have something special for you. They brought it to me yesterday, but I couldn't get to the barrack to give it to you."

I scrunched up my forehead, perplexed. We had requested a few more films for the children, some fruit and other items, but I got the impression Elisabeth was not referring to anything like that.

"What is it? Don't keep me in suspense!"

"Here," she said, handing me a piece of paper with handwriting on it.

My heart skipped a beat. It had to be news about Johann. I had not given up all hope, but over the last few weeks I had been trying not to harbor any illusions.

My eyes devoured the hastily written words. There was just a name, Kanada, and my husband's personal information.

"He's in Kanada?" I asked, confused. I had thought there were only about a thousand workers there and that they were all very young men and women.

"Yes. First he was in one of the exterior work groups, living outside of Birkenau, but he's been in Kanada for a month now. Things in Auschwitz never follow any logic, but you must be relieved. Work groups assigned there eat well, have good clothes, and their work is not as hard as many others," Elisabeth explained.

Since my arrival at camp, I had worked hard to learn as little as possible about the inner workings of Auschwitz, but unfortunately it had become a well-known secret that most of the thousands of people who arrived day after day by train were sent to the gas chambers at the back of the camp and then their bodies were incinerated. All of their belongings were taken to Kanada, where the prisoners had nearly everything at their disposal, including clothing, hats, shoes, glasses, leg braces, suitcases, and any other object the poor victims had brought. Though the Nazis were primarily interested in the gold and money the Jews brought sewn into their clothes, they took advantage of everything. The German population that was suffering greatly because of the war, the mutilated and injured, the orphans and widows—they all received the belongings of the thousands and thousands of victims from Birkenau's death factory.

"He's alive and so close," I whispered in a sigh.

"Woman, you've just learned that your husband has survived among ten thousand dead men, and that's all you can say?"

"How can I see him or communicate with him?" I asked anxiously.

"I can get a message to him, but seeing him would have to be authorized by an officer. You must have a pass to go to other sections of the camp," Elisabeth said.

I walked back to the children's school hardly feeling the ground beneath my feet. I was elated. I did not stop to see the children who had not shown up for class that day, but I did want to go to the hospital. I needed to tell someone. I went into barrack 26 and looked for Ludwika. She was the person I was closest to at the camp, though our friendship was unlike any other I had experienced before Auschwitz. The circumstances that had brought us together were so adverse that it was hard to tell if we were actually friends or just cosufferers who needed each other.

As soon as she saw my face, the Polish nurse knew that something was going on. She asked one of her colleagues to take over what she had been working on and walked the length of the barrack toward me. For a few seconds I studied the dozens of patients resting on the cots that were very similar to what they had in the regular barracks. I knew through the doctors and nurses that there were hardly any medicines available. Patients had to get better and heal on the strength of rest alone, but for many, that was not enough. Mengele had given the order that any invalid who needed to stay in the hospital longer than five days was to be selected for elimination. He never made the selections directly in the hospital, but the doctors followed his orders. I went up to the bed of a seven-year-old girl who had been one of our students in the past few weeks. A simple outbreak of chicken pox had sent her to bed. Her body did not have enough defenses to fight it. Fortunately, we had detected it in time before it spread to the rest of the children.

"Hello, Jadzia. How are you feeling today?" I asked, stroking her head.

"Good, Teacher," she said weakly.

Her face was covered in sores, her body was wasted away, and her cadaverous face looked at me with angelic innocence. I had to glance away before I started to cry. Despite everything I had seen at Auschwitz, I was still unable to keep from crying when I looked at a dying child.

"We'll be right back, Jadzia," Ludwika said when she got to the foot of the cot.

She took me by the arm and led me out to the hot August sunshine, which actually seemed cool compared to the suffocating atmosphere of the hospital barrack.

"How is she?" I asked about the girl.

"The doctors have selected her. They'll take her this afternoon." Ludwika's eyes were clouded with pain.

We were silent for a few seconds, staring at the sky and the huge train station. It was full of new arrivals that morning. Often we tried to ignore the trains in the pointless attempt to forget about the destiny of those poor new-comers.

"It's terrible," I said at last, the words hurting as they left my lips.

"Everything here is. We can maybe save one or two out of every hundred. Getting sick is a death sentence," Ludwika answered.

"Yes, I hope none of the other children caught it." This was a real concern for me. I was thinking of my own children but also of every boy and girl who came to the nursery and school. We had all grown attached to them.

"We'll have to wait at least a week. This virus can take awhile to show up. But today is a day to celebrate. It's the twins' birthday, isn't it?" Her voice had adopted an excited tone.

At that moment, a birthday celebration sounded like a bad idea. How could I put on a party that afternoon while they murdered Jadzia?

"Yes, the twins turn seven today. They are so thin."

"We're all thin. The important thing is that they're not sick," Ludwika said.

"Yes, it's true. Well, there's something else . . . Johann is apparently in Kanada."

"Kanada? That's incredible. You've been less than a mile apart all this time and didn't even know it." She was smiling incredulously.

"Yes. Elisabeth will get a note to him to let him know we're all right, but the only way I can see him is with permission from an officer."

"But you could ask Mengele! You know you're one of his favorites. After all, you're not a Jew or a Gypsy, and you've never been a Communist. I'm sure he'd grant you permission."

"You think so?" I asked nervously.

"Definitely. He's very upbeat today; I saw him just an hour ago. Apparently his wife is here. You know he never talks about anything personal, but he was particularly happy today."

I had to seize the opportunity. The doctor had a rather fickle temperament. When the day was gray or things were complicated, he became very taciturn and moody.

"You think now is a good time?" My voice cracked with my excitement.

She nodded. "He's in the sauna, in his laboratory. He deals with correspondence the first part of the day and hasn't yet started with his experiments, which take up the rest of the day."

"Well, I want to try right now. The best gift I could give my children is for them to see their father." In my euphoria, my heart felt like it was going to beat out of my chest.

"Okay, then, go on. What are you waiting for?" Ludwika nudged me.

I went down the stairs and walked down the dusty road toward the sauna. It felt like a long walk though it was only seven barracks away. When I came up to number 34, doubts started crowding my thoughts. I was about to turn around and walk away, but I realized I had nothing to lose. I was the director of the nursery school, and Mengele knew I was doing a good job. He could undoubtedly find someone to take my place, but I had learned early on that he did not like change. He wanted things to clip along with continuity and routine so that nothing interrupted his experiments.

Finally, I went up the three stairs and knocked softly at the door. I was unsure if I had been heard. Again, I was about to turn around and head back, but then I heard a voice from the other side telling me to come in.

I opened the door slowly. There was little light in the room. It was long but not very wide. On one side was the doctor's desk, with a bookshelf behind it full of files; on the other side a hospital bed for observing patients. Next to the bed was a white cabinet with instruments and medicines.

The doctor looked up, clearly puzzled to see me. I was about to excuse myself and leave, but I made myself stay calmly rooted in place a few feet from his desk, waiting for him to speak.

"Frau Hannemann, to what do I owe this pleasant surprise? I was not expecting you. Is there a problem with the children?" he asked, his brows knitted together.

Though his concern seemed genuine, he never ceased to surprise me. How was it possible for him to feel such affection for the children and yet be capable of sending them to their deaths over a simple illness?

"No, Herr Doktor, I've come about a personal matter." I could not keep the nervousness from my voice.

"I see. You have never asked me for anything for yourself before. I imagine it is something very important. I see you as a good German mother, a true model for our race. I have told my wife, Irene, about you, and she has asked to come see the nursery school this afternoon," Mengele said.

I had not expected him to say that. We had never seen the wife of any Nazi in the camp, but Mengele was not the average SS member. Where others were barbaric and cold, he was always calm and polite.

"It would be an honor to have her," I said.

"I won't be taking her anywhere else in the camp; it's no place for a lady."

I was again surprised. Were we not mothers, wives, ladies like Irene? Every day thousands of women, children, and elderly people died, but to the Nazis we were merely a tattooed number, a statistic in a notebook of entries and exits.

Mengele went on, "In the women's camp, there's been a typhus outbreak, but thankfully the Gypsy camp is at quite a distance from the primary locus. She'll be here hardly an hour and then I'll take her back." He seemed to be trying to convince himself that his wife would not be in danger if she came to visit us.

"We're having a party in two hours."

"Perfect, we'll come then. You know that when a woman gets a notion in her head, it's impossible to convince her otherwise. But what was it you wanted to see me about?" he asked, looking back down at his papers.

I clammed up. Maybe it was not a good time. He seemed busy and also worried about his wife. I was working up the nerve to open my mouth when he said, "Come on, out with it."

"They've found my husband. He's in Kanada. I wanted to ask you for permission to see him. This is the first news I've had of him since we arrived in May." It tumbled forth in a rush, like I wanted to throw it all out at once and run away to safety.

"Very well. I'll write you a pass to go to Kanada. You'll have an hour after the party. I'm not sure they'll let you see him alone, but I won't be able to allow this to happen again. Personal relationships distract my assistants from their work. You have been loyal, and I want you to know

I appreciate it, but the work comes first. Is that clear?" he asked with his freezing stare.

"Yes, Herr Doktor," I said, swallowing hard.

He took out a piece of paper with letterhead, wrote for a few seconds, sealed it, then handed it to me.

"One hour, and not a minute more," he said, looking me straight in the eyes.

"Yes, Herr Doktor."

My heart was bursting out of my chest as I left his laboratory. The children could not see their father after all; in fact, I planned on not saying anything about it until the next day so they would not get worked up. But when they found out that he was all right and only a few hundred yards away, surely they would be pleased.

In the nursery barrack, excitement had taken hold of all the little hearts. It was the first party to be held in the camp, and though we could not offer anything grand, thanks to everyone's cooperation we had managed to bake a simple cake and cover it in chocolate. It was a true delicacy for everyone who came.

I warned the children that in an hour Dr. Mengele's wife would be coming and that they should treat her with utmost respect and kindness. We aired out the barracks to thin the stench of sweat and diapers. The Gypsy mothers took all the children outside to play while Kasandra, Maja,

Zelma, and I decorated the room for the party. We made colored paper chains and had managed to acquire some balloons and streamers. We were all properly excited by the time we finished, and for a moment I had forgotten about my upcoming visit to Johann.

We lined all the children up between the barracks and waited in the shade for the doctor to arrive with his wife. After an hour, they still had not shown up. I figured Mengele had finally thought better of the idea. He knew his wife might be affected by what she saw in the camp, so I intuited that they would not be coming.

The children were hot, tired, and impatient to start the party. We let them into the building and were delighted to see their wide eyes and surprised faces as they looked at the decorations. Emily and Ernest were so happy I could hardly blink back my tears.

"Let's start the games," I told a group of children, who immediately started screaming and jumping up and down.

For that hour, we traveled to a place very far away from the barbed-wire fences. The children hunted after treasure, discovered hidden secrets, listened to a story, and watched an improvised puppet show put on by the teachers. I had never seen them so happy, but the biggest surprise of all was when we turned off the lights and I came out with the cake lit with two candles. The twins stared at each other with their jaws dropped. I placed the cake on the table and hugged them.

"Everybody get together," I said to all the children. They all scrambled right up against the twins, who had knelt down to blow out the candles. I would have liked to take their picture, though I did not want them to remember this place when they were older.

"Have you made a wish?" I asked.

"Yes!" they answered in unison.

"Don't tell anybody what it was, so it can come true," I warned them.

Heedless of my words, Ernest blurted out, "We want Daddy to be okay, and we want to see him!"

That stopped me in my tracks. It was only for a few seconds, but images of recent birthdays flashed before my eyes. Johann had always been there. This was the first birthday he had missed.

"Blow out the candles!" I said, hastily wiping the tears that had started to flow.

The twins blew them out, and we all started singing. The room filled with the innocent voices of nearly one hundred children, and the whole camp heard their song. We were celebrating life in the middle of a graveyard. It almost seemed sacrilegious to me, but then I thought that as long as children can sing, the world still has a chance. Their voices filled our souls, which by then were as emaciated as our bodies. Evil moved with such strength in Auschwitz that it seemed like a dry, sterile land where everything good withered sooner or later. I knew that a nursery school in the middle of the horror could not be the exception to the rule. Even so, I tried to enjoy what each day offered us. One candle for each year of life. In Auschwitz-Birkenau we should have blown out a candle for every hour and every minute. A year was an unimaginable length of time.

TWELVE

AUGUST 1943
AUSCHWITZ

I had a hard time justifying to my children my need to be absent. I did not want to tell them I was going to see their father, because they could not come with me. The twins were still high on the excitement of their birthday party, and they were so worked up about the little carved wooden horse I had given them that they hardly noticed I was going to leave. Adalia was too exhausted to protest much, but the two older children did not let me get away easily. They peppered me with questions until I left them with Zelma and her children and headed to the entrance of the Gypsy camp.

The walk down the main road felt longer than usual. I would have to get through at least three checkpoints, and though I had a letter of safe conduct from Dr. Mengele, that did not guarantee that the guards would let me through. When I came up to the office barracks, I looked from side to side to make sure neither of the feared female guards were there. Fortunately for me, at that hour of the day they were at the train station helping with the selection of new prisoners.

I had never gone so close to the exit before. My breath came in quick, short gasps as I stopped in front of the main gate. For several months now those fences had become the worst sort of prison home for me.

The soldier on guard spoke harshly. "What is it?"

I expected no tact. To them I was at best a number but more likely just rubbish to be trampled.

"Dr. Mengele has written me a pass to visit Kanada," I said, holding out the paper. My voice and my hands trembled.

The soldier held his gun with one hand while he took the letter in the other and went to the guardhouse where they sat when it rained or snowed. A sergeant came out of the small wooden building and approached me.

"Everything's in order, but it'll be dark within an hour. You must be back before the sun goes down."

I sighed with relief, nodded, and took the paper back. As I walked through the gate, I was instantaneously aware of two things. The first was my physical appearance: it had been a very long time since I had seen a mirror, colored my gray roots, or tamed the wild hairs around my temples.

Though I had cut my hair, I undoubtedly looked wretched. I knew my face would be sunken in with bags under my eyes, the nurse's smock I was wearing was old and shabby, and the toes of my shoes were open holes. I pulled a pink ribbon out of one of the pockets of my smock and tried to tame my blonde mane into a ponytail. I pinched my cheeks to brighten my pallor and set off for Kanada at a brisk pace. The second thing I was aware of was that in the camp no one was called by name. I would have to search among the thousand-some-odd people of the Kanada work commandos. It would take me too long and would drastically reduce my chances of finding my husband; and if by some miracle I did locate him, we would barely have any time to talk.

The huge road was completely empty. Large watchtowers interrupted the monotonous landscape of wire fences and barracks behind them. I went by the gate that led to the camp hospital and stopped at another checkpoint. There were many more soldiers here than at the Gypsy camp. Kanada held true treasures robbed from the murdered prisoners. I showed my letter to the sergeant and they let me enter one of the least accessible areas of Birkenau. I walked between two huge buildings with smokestacks, crematoriums 4 and 5, respectively. I did not dawdle. Turning the corner of one of the crematoriums, I found myself at the entrance to Kanada.

Since our arrival in Auschwitz I had heard all sorts of

rumors about that place. Most of them turned out to be true. What first took me off guard was how immensely large it was. It was twice as wide as our camp, though not as deep. There were dozens of barracks laid out in rows. The ones at the back were stuffed with clothes, shoes, and suitcases waiting to be sorted. Given the good weather and the ceaseless arrivals of trains that summer, the workers could not keep up with their macabre work.

I showed my letter to the guards at the entrance and they allowed me to enter with no problem. I looked for a few seconds longer at what were at least fifty barracks and sank again into despair. It seemed impossible to find Johann in a place like that in such a short time. My only chance was to ask people about him, hoping that there were not many Gypsies in Kanada.

I saw a young woman dressed in pants and wearing makeup. Her hair was very tidy. I asked, "Excuse me, where are the men's barracks?"

I was surprised at how healthy she looked and how normal her clothes seemed. In fact, most people I saw there looked healthy and reasonably well dressed, not wearing tattered rags like the rest of us prisoners. She looked me over nonchalantly and pointed carelessly to the barracks to my right. Then she disappeared into the mountain of objects at the door of one of them. I walked as quickly as

I could toward the men's barracks. I went up to one of the first buildings and found a man in his forties with dark hair who was wearing an old but elegant suit.

"I'm looking for a Gypsy man named Johann. He plays the violin," I explained. I wondered if Kanada also had an orchestra; if so, Johann perhaps might have joined it.

"A Gypsy?" The man said the word like it tasted bad in his mouth. "I haven't seen any around here."

I continued my desperate search, glancing frequently at the sky to see how the sun was little by little making its way toward the forest on the far horizon. *Don't give up*, I said, resorting to entering the barracks and calling out Johann's name. I was so close to reaching my goal that I could not give up now. I had to see him even if it were for the very last time.

I asked after him in two or three barracks but to no avail. I ran around stopping every man I came across to ask. I was about to call the search off when I ran into a boy who could not have been more than fifteen years old. He had his hat pulled down low over his head and was wearing a kind of work uniform and military boots that were too big.

"Frau, I know a Gypsy. He's in barrack 45, but right now he's working on the train platform. Some of us go there to pick up the bags after the selections," he explained.

I was ready to throw myself down and sob like a child. I tried to get myself together and just be grateful that Johann was alive. But I could not believe the irony of being here when he was not. The opportunity was slipping between my fingers.

"Could you please give him this?" I asked, handing the boy the letter I had managed to write a few hours before.

"Of course, Frau."

I thanked him and headed for the exit. My bad luck dumbfounded me, though on the other hand I knew I should not complain. Almost everyone still alive in Auschwitz had lost everyone they loved shortly after arriving at the camp, and at least my whole family was still breathing.

I was walking out of the first round of fencing when I saw a large group of men carrying suitcases approaching. I paused to see if Johann was among them. The special work group entering Kanada was escorted by soldiers and kapos. I walked through the rows impatiently but saw no sign of him. Desperate, I started shouting his name.

"Frau, you can't be here," a kapo reprimanded me, pushing me away with a nightstick.

"Please, I have a letter of safe passage. My husband is here, Johann the Gypsy." My words came out with rapid-fire anxiety.

Then all the prisoners started yelling Johann's name, the choruses running the length of the rows of workers. A second later, a man stepped away from the ranks. He looked to be at least fifty years old. He was wearing a plain violet-colored shirt and dark pants that hung loosely off his extremely thin frame.

"Helene!" the man yelled in an unmistakable voice. My knees buckled as I heard my name from his lips, and I began to weep.

We ran and caught each other in a long embrace. We hardly said a word. Two halves have no need for speech to become a whole again. There in front of them all we kissed unabashedly, the guards and kapos looking on in shock. We represented everyone's life right then, the days when each of those men walked free in the world before becoming executioners, victims, ghosts.

"It's the twins' birthday today," he said, our tearstained faces pressed against each other.

"Yes, yes, they're all fine and miss you so much."

"Good God, I thought I had lost you all forever," he said between heaving sobs.

I held him tightly, feeling his pronounced ribs and sweaty skin. I could smell his essence. I took his face in my hands and concentrated all my energy on burning his image into my retinas. He was still beautiful to me despite being battered by life. His sunken cheeks, his face scraggly with intermittent shaving, the dimple in his chin, his bushy eyebrows, his gray-streaked dark hair brushed back—it was the beautiful face of the man I loved. In that moment I would have thrown it all away for him, even my own children. It was incomprehensible to any but a woman in love who had just found her long-lost beloved. When you find the one you love, everything inside is on fire. The half of you that was destroyed and abandoned fits together again, and pain and suffering become ghosts from the long-distant past. I wanted to touch his face, kiss his lips, be soothed by his long musician's fingers: to be his wife, one flesh and one blood.

Those were the only minutes in Auschwitz that flew by. Inside the fence, time crept by with unnatural slowness, but the hands of the watch raced against one another there with Johann, compelled by Cronus's eternal fear of Aphrodite.

The sun was setting. The shadows were growing longer. Our hands fought to stay entwined as I began to lean away, back toward the crematoriums.

"Will I see you again?" His question was that of a dreaming man to a vision. His eyes pulsed with pain, and I rushed to kiss him again. It was fleeing, like a breath of fresh wind in the desert, but it was enough to carry me back to the heavy burden destiny had assigned me: guarding the labyrinth and preparing the Minotaur his daily offerings of death and pain.

I did not want to lie. I let the silence answer his doubts. Our fingers brushed against each other one last time, and an electric shock jolted me from the tips of each digit. I walked backward as long as I could. The work group began to stumble toward Kanada, everyone hypnotized by what they had just witnessed. Love did not exist in Auschwitz, and if it ever managed to grow up among the putrid waste of the streets, it quickly withered under the camp's scorching hatred.

As I walked blindly toward the second checkpoint, I felt like I had left my soul behind. I could not fight off the sensation of emptiness, dry and hollow inside. I tried to cheer myself up with fake hope, but I did not believe my own lies. I walked as briskly as I could down the road. I no longer feared the guards. Maternal instinct drove me, the need to get back to my pups and nestle them beside me. When I got to the Gypsy camp, I felt like I was once again entering the mouth of hell. I wanted to give up, throw in the towel. But I had to be strong. There were nearly a hundred children depending on me, not to mention my own sons and daughters and the women in my charge. One little error could destroy everything we had painstakingly built. Yet in that moment all I felt was a gaping emptiness.

The road through camp was empty since it was forbidden to go outside the barracks after sundown. The guards verified my pass, and ten minutes later I was at the nursery school. The three youngest were already in bed. My friend Ludwika interrogated me with her eyes but said nothing. I forced the pain away, got Blaz and Otis in bed, left the door cracked, and went to sit beside her.

MARIO ESCOBAR

"Did you see him?"

"Yes," I answered, trying to swallow back my tears through the lump in my throat. "I was about to give up when he came back with his work group. It was just a few minutes, but I could touch him and kiss him."

"I am so, so glad," she said very seriously.

In a way, I was being selfish. All the prisoners here in Auschwitz had a sad story to tell and someone they loved, lost forever in the sky over Poland. Ludwika had her share of pain as well. Suddenly, she flinched and seemed to come out of some flash of memory. She grabbed my hand.

"Don't give up. You're doing something truly beautiful with these children. Ever since you came, a ray of hope has penetrated the camp. You may not realize it, but you're an inspiration and a hope for all of us. Look what you've accomplished in just a few months"—she waved her hand around the nursery—"but this is only the beginning. The storm is still to come. The war isn't going well for the Germans, and I don't know how they'll react when they realize they're about to lose. I fear the worst, which is why it's important to have people like you to lead the way."

"I'm nobody, Ludwika. I'm just a poor mother trying to take care of her children," I answered.

"No, Helene. God sent you here to guide us. We needed a breath of hope, and you showed up with your beautiful

182

family. I've never known anyone as brave and determined as you." She gave me a hug.

Sometimes we have to lose everything to find what is most important. When life robs us of what we thought we could not live without and leaves us standing naked before reality, the essential things that had always been invisible take on their true value.

"You make me feel proud again to belong to the human race, Helene Hannemann."

Those words filled my lungs with the air I had lost in Kanada when I had to walk away from Johann.

"As long as I'm alive and have the strength, I will do everything possible to get them to treat us like human beings. It won't be easy, but we'll do our best not to ever lose our dignity," I said.

My friend stood up with her chin raised. She had recovered some of the pride she had lost when she arrived at Auschwitz. I could see the fear receding from her eyes. That was the Nazis' true weapon, domination by inflicting terror.

Months later, I remembered the words of that conversation. My friend had been right. The storm was approaching at the end of the summer, though for a while we thought it would pass and that our ship would not sink to the depths of the Nazi extermination camps.

THIRTEEN

OCTOBER 1943
AUSCHWITZ

As we had thought, things got slowly but steadily worse over the summer. It was now widely known that the Nazis were starting to lose the war. News of big losses on the Russian front trickled in slowly, as did news of Allied advances in Italy and the destruction of the greater part of the German air fleet. Since summer had begun to fade, German cities had been bombed regularly, and every day we heard bomber planes flying overhead. Things were not getting any better in Auschwitz. The guards were on edge because of the downturn in the war; and a new inspector, Konrad Morgen, had been sent from Berlin. After his arrival, even Dr. Mengele was more jittery.

We did not see Mengele around the Gypsy camp as

much. He spent most of his time on the train platforms and in the hospital barracks, where he had taken most of the twins for his experiments. No one knew what he wanted with the poor creatures, though some people said his goal was to make German mothers more fertile so they could fill the earth with their offspring. For the Nazis, women were baby factories. The only thing they cared about was our fertility. We were supposed to produce strong, healthy children for the Reich, which would then take and throw them into the conflagration of the war. How many good boys had died for their leader on the Russian steppes or in the African deserts?

Mengele dreamed of supplying the machine of Nazi destruction with an endless supply of innocent creatures with clear blue eyes and straw-blonde hair. He had also seemed to lose interest in the nursery and school. Despite my repeated requests for the materials we needed for the children, he would only send a formal letter to the camp commandant, or he would just ignore me. We had become the broken toy, no longer holding any appeal for him.

I tried to face the problems with a positive attitude and not think much about the future.

Despite the widespread problems and general deterioration at the camp, a few weeks earlier, an older gentleman named Antonin Strnad had, with the guards' permission, started a school for older boys. Blaz attended, balancing the classes with afternoon rehearsals for the Gypsy orchestra. The rest of the time he helped me in the nursery and with the younger children in the evening.

One Sunday my son was on edge. Some of the camp officers were coming that day to listen to our orchestra, and the players were keenly aware of how dangerous it could be if the Nazis were displeased with the performance. I intended to take advantage of the visit of the officers to beg them to provide the supplies we needed to take care of the children.

The camp commandant arrived with the other officers just before noon. We had had a week with no rain, but other prisoners told me that as soon as November began, the weather in Auschwitz would be brutal: relentless rain, snow, and cold that seeped into your bones.

The visiting party sat on chairs we had set up beside one of the first barracks at the camp. All the prisoners were edgy because of the visit, but after threats and blows from the kapos, they settled down. The younger prisoners sat while the older ones stood to listen to the concert.

When the music started to flow that chilly Sunday morning, for a few moments we all forgot about the difficult conditions of the last few weeks and allowed the ethereal notes to transport us far away. I closed my eyes for a few moments and disassociated from where I was. Light gently penetrated my closed eyelids, and I felt a momentary peace. The beautiful sounds seemed to have the same effect on both executioners and victims. Their evil did not negate the fact that they were also tormented souls. They had gone belly-up in the ocean of disdain and little by little drowned in their own cruelty.

When I opened my eyes again, it was to behold the beautiful picture of my son playing the violin with impressive skill. He was Johann from years ago: the same simple elegance and relaxed posture as if his feet did not rest on earthly ground. The violin sang sadly in his hands and dexterously drew out all the feelings we had been repressing for months.

Mengele was not far from me. The prisoners had brought seats for the medical staff as well, and each time I turned my head, I could see his enraptured face. In the few months I had known him, he had undergone a drastic change. It reminded me of Oscar Wilde's *The Picture of Dorian Gray*. The protagonist sells his soul to the devil in exchange for retaining his youth and beauty, but though he remains externally attractive, over time he deteriorates internally, which is apparent in a picture he keeps locked up in his room. Eventually the picture shows the portrait of a monster.

I had never realized this before about Mengele, or had not been able to verbalize it. I was terrified of him. I recalled the morning not long ago when Zosia, one of Mengele's assistants with his experiments, came to the school to pick up a set of twins. I walked her to the door, and as soon as we were outside she told the two girls to go up the road a bit. Then she put her hands to her face and broke down crying.

"I can't do it anymore. If I had known what that madman does with the poor little things . . . Every day I wake up telling myself this will be the last time I have to assist him," she cried. "The first thing I think about when I get up is throwing myself against the electric fence and ending it all, but I don't have the courage."

"It won't be much longer, Zosia. The Allies will come soon and get us out of here," I said, trying to comfort her.

"But until they get here, he's still a monster; he'll torture hundreds every week . . ."

Her words were perplexing, and they chilled me to the bone. There were plenty of rumors about what went on in the sauna and in barrack 14 of the hospital, which some called the Zoo, but hearing it firsthand from one of the doctor's assistants made my heart skip a beat.

"Every day we carry out experiments on children of all ages. First we research and then do trials to try to change their eye color. So many have died from infections or have been left blind. Now we're infecting the children with all sorts of diseases to kill them later and do autopsies. It's horrible! I can't do it anymore!"

I hugged her while the twins waited a short distance away. I looked at them. Elena and Josephine were two beautiful little Jewish girls who had been selected by the doctor shortly after their arrival. They usually slept in the orphans' barrack, but I already knew that once children were officially requested by the doctor, they never returned to the nursery school or to the Gypsy camp at all. They stayed in the hospital barrack 14. At first Mengele only sent for twins sporadically, but since August, a steady stream of one or two pairs of twins per week had left our camp and never returned. The supply of new pairs of twins had dwindled since September, and every day I was terrified that the doctor would ask for my own children for his experiments.

My chest was hurting. I took a deep breath and hugged Zosia again, who recommended her tears. I held her as she wept for a few minutes. Then she pulled herself together, dried her tears, and said she was much better. She went off holding each girl by the hand and swinging her arms with theirs, and I hated Mengele from the bottom of my heart. I hated him and all the Nazis there at the camp. They murdered our bodies but also corrupted our souls, stealing the most precious part of us, our very humanity.

When the concert was over, I approached the doctor. He was talking with other officers and pretended not to notice me. I stayed patiently by his side, determined to ask him to improve our situation in the nursery school. Yet I grew more nervous as the minutes passed. Finally, he turned, looked me up and down with his freezing eyes, and smiled softly.

"It seems you have something important to say, prisoner?"

"Yes, Herr Doktor," I stuttered.

"I have received your reports and requests. I am doing what I can, but things have changed notably in the past few months. The bombings from the Marxists and Jews are getting worse." He frowned. "Thousands of German children are homeless and practically starving. You don't want us to stop feeding German mouths in order to fill the bellies of Jewish rats and lowly races?"

I knew it would be imprudent to answer that question, but rage was building from my stomach to my mouth. I took a deep breath, forced a calm into my voice, and said, "I understand. But we have no more milk, the rations are extremely scarce, and most of the children are getting sick. Half of them won't make it through the winter."

"Well, then that's fewer mouths to feed. Don't forget it: the strongest survive. It's simply natural selection." He was indifferent.

"They are locked up and have no chance of survival. This is not natural selection; it's letting them die of starvation, exposure to the elements, and misery." I had not controlled my growing fury.

"Watch your tone! Until now I've tolerated your impertinence because you're a German woman of the Aryan race, but my patience has its limits. Remember that you have five mouths to feed. Worry about them, not all the Gypsies. What do you care what happens to the rest of them? What I receive from the Kaiser Wilhelm Institute is barely enough for me to feed the children in barrack 14 at the hospital. I can't maintain all the Gypsies at Birkenau; I'm not their father."

He was losing his temper. As Mengele spoke, he drew closer and closer to me, spluttering with rage. I pulled back, shaking with fear and anger. I had never seen him so upset. The rest of the officers turned to see what was going on. Mengele realized and calmed down immediately.

"This is not the place to discuss such a sensitive issue. I'll see you in my office at five o'clock. Do be on time. I want to close this subject for good." His tone was soft and his demeanor calm, but rage boiled underneath. Then he turned from me and flashed his smile at the rest of the officers, a completely different person again: the enchanting Josef, the quintessential conversation partner and bamboozler of women.

I took my children by the hand and started back toward the nursery barrack. I wanted to get as far away as possible from him. Zelma followed and caught up with me before we got to the barrack. She put her hand on my shoulder and, with a sad face, asked, "What did the doctor tell you?"

"He wants to see me later," I answered shortly, not wanting to go into details.

"Five more children have died this week. At this pace we'll lose half of them before January." She winced at the thought.

"I know. I think about it every minute of every day. It tortures me. Like I said, I'll do what I can to try to help the situation, but it won't be easy." Inside, though, I was working hard to convince myself to keep trying, to hold nothing back in attempting to convince Mengele that we were still worth keeping alive.

"I will pray for you. It's not easy to make deals with the devil," Zelma answered. Then she turned and walked away, her head down low.

While the orchestra dispersed, the prisoners returned to their daily routines of death and horror. In the last few months, nearly all the Gypsy families had lost at least one or two of their loved ones. The first victims had been the babies. Since we had been at the camp, over two hundred had been born, but only 20 percent survived past the first week. Then the young children started dying because of malnutrition and chronic diarrhea, which left most of them so weak that a light cold snuffed out their frail lives in a heartbeat. The adults had also started to disappear little by little. For the Nazis the increased deaths were a relief: fewer mouths to feed.

"Mom, are we going?" Blaz's question shook me from my thoughts.

"Yes, sorry. Let's head back to our barrack. You played so well this morning. Maybe your father even heard you through the fence. Kanada isn't far from here, and the wind can carry the sound several hundred yards," I said, forcing a cheeriness. But Blaz could read me better than anyone else and knew I was worried about our family and the rest of the camp's children.

The morning after I had seen Johann, I told the children about the brief encounter I had had with their father on the day of the twins' birthday. They all started complaining that I had not taken them with me, except Blaz. He understood perfectly well that I would have taken them if it had at all been within my power.

"The one thing I don't like is having to play in front of all those people. They're evil, Mom. Our professor, Mr. Antonin, has told us what they do with the people in the buildings with the chimneys. They kill them. Women, little kids, and old people, they all suffocate to death, day after day."

I listened, horrified. I had known that sooner or later he would learn what happened to all the people who arrived on the trains, but it terrified me to think how this horror was affecting his developing brain. An eleven-year-old boy is not ready to handle certain things or to face what Blaz had been forced to experience in Auschwitz.

"Please don't talk about that with anyone. We have to survive, Blaz. Our only hope is to hold out 'til the end of the war. But to survive, we have to slip under the radar and go unnoticed."

The rest of the children came up then and interrupted our conversation. The minutes dragged by that day. In a few hours I would have to face Mengele again, and the mere thought of entering his laboratory gave me goose bumps. I had always been conscious of the fact that my life was in his hands, but now my greatest fear was what he might do to my children.

Ludwika came to the nursery barrack a few minutes before five o'clock. I jumped at the sound of her knock even though it could not be Mengele. He would not have come to see us personally. She tried to calm me down. The children sensed that something was wrong and fluttered around me constantly, like terrified chicks not wanting to stray far from their mother. Ludwika grabbed my arm and pulled me out into the cool afternoon.

"You need to primp a little bit. Put some lipstick on and act natural, unconcerned," she said, handing me a tube of lipstick.

"Are you mad? Do you think I'm going to go flirt with him?" I answered furiously. How could my friend suggest such a wretched proposal?

"I don't mean seduce him; he's already got a lover. Everyone knows that since his wife left, he's been sleeping with Irma Grese. That sadist is a demon, but apparently demons attract demons."

Something about her comment bothered me. I knew she was right, but even in Mengele's worst moments I had detected something human in him. Undoubtedly wrong and heartless, but still human. The nature of the female guards, though, was pure fiend.

I took my friend's advice and smoothed down my hair, put the lipstick on, and then headed for Mengele's laboratory with a decided step. I had married very young, and my experience with men had been so limited that I would not have known how to seduce one if I wanted to, though I had learned that it did not take much for the male gender to fall to the wiles of a female.

I took a deep breath before knocking and entered the sauna barrack without waiting for a reply. The doctor was at his desk drinking a soft drink. I had never seen him drink alcohol, though the rest of the camp guards and officers felt no need to abstain. His jacket was unbuttoned, and he looked down in the dumps. I was taken aback to see him like that, as his countenance in no way reflected the arrogant man I had argued with a few hours before. Otto Rosenberg, one of the older Gypsy boys who waited on Mengele at the camp, always said the doctor spent most of his time absorbed in his experiments or staring off into space through the dirty windows of the barrack.

"Frau Hannemann, please, come in and have a seat," he said with as much charm and politeness as when he had first asked me to discuss the idea of the nursery school.

"Thank you, Herr Doktor," I replied coolly and sat down.

"I apologize for how I behaved this morning," he began. "The volume of work increases day by day, and the resources grow ever scarcer. I would like to focus on my experiments, but the trains come one after the other, and I have to spend most of my time on the platform. It's a difficult but necessary job. Most of those poor devils wouldn't last a day in Birkenau."

"I'm sorry about your situation, but I assure you that

the children of the Gypsy camp are on the brink of death. They are frightfully thin and are falling ill."

"I know; I'm their doctor. Though now I'm required to spend more and more time in the general hospital for the entire camp. I can assure you we are concerned for the Gypsy children, but it is not easy to get help," he said, getting to his feet. I knew that was a lie. He did not give a fig for any of us, but Nazi doublespeak always played behind his ambiguous, meaningless words.

He walked through the room until he was standing just behind me. I could not see him, but my body sensed his proximity. He always smelled of cologne, and his uniform gave off the smell of machine-washed officer clothes. I was beginning to understand that for many Nazis, the first few years in Auschwitz had been like an extended summer camp that was slowly drawing to an end.

"I will ask the commandant himself to send milk, bread, and other foodstuffs to the nursery, as well as the necessary school supplies. The doctors have told me about an illness that many of the Gypsy children are presenting. It's called noma. Have you heard of it?"

I turned to look at him. It was true that Dr. Senkteller and Ludwika had told me that some of the children had a strange disease on their faces and genitals. The cases had increased lately, and after the scarcities that fall, many of the children had a kind of bloody ulcer on their faces. I was terrified that my own children would catch it, but so far none of them had.

"Noma is a disease endemic to Africa, and there have been no cases in Europe until now. It is a polymicrobial gangrenous infection in the mouth and genitals. There are many causes, but predisposing conditions include unsanitary living conditions and a lack of vitamins A and B. Normally it affects children under twelve years of age, and the mortality rate is very high, up to ninety-five percent of those who fall ill."

I sucked in my breath. Up to now, there had been few serious cases, but I could not believe the disease would be that deadly.

"That's why I've decided not to let the twins return to the nursery or the school. I'm afraid they'll contract the disease," Mengele explained.

"But is it contagious?" I asked. I vaguely recalled having heard about the disease during nursing school, but at the time I had never seen a case.

"We don't think so. It can be stopped with antibiotics and an enriched diet. I cannot guarantee a supply of the former, as most of the medicines are sent to the front or to our cities being bombed daily by the Brits and the Americans, but we can partially improve the diet of your students."

"But, Herr Doktor, diet won't be enough."

"I'm researching noma with Dr. Berthold Epstein, and I hope to find a more effective cure as soon as possible. That's why we've transferred some of the children, especially the more serious cases, to the camp hospital," he continued.

I stood. At least I had managed to get him to agree to improve some aspects of the living conditions of the Gypsy children in our camp.

"Don't be alarmed if we take some of the healthy children as well. We believe that noma has a hereditary component. Gypsies are an endogamous people. The syphilis that many of the men have seems to be related to a predisposition to the disease. For example, in the Czech family camp there have hardly been any cases." His voice was matter-of-fact.

"But they haven't been here very long," I said.

We had heard that the Nazis had allowed the Czech Jews to live in a family camp. That was the great exception in Auschwitz, though most assumed it was a way to appease the voices outside of Germany that were rising up against the mistreatment of Jews.

The doctor smiled at me, and I could see the gap between his big front teeth. He looked like a harmless, mischievous youth incapable of causing actual damage, but he had lost his power to trick me with his soft words and polite manners.

"I will work with you as long as you keep your word to improve conditions for the children. Please, don't forget that they are human beings just like us. They may not have Aryan blood, but it is still blood, Herr Doktor."

Creases appeared in his forehead, and his expression changed instantly. For a moment I feared that I had gone too far. But I also sensed that Mengele respected me for being able to say exactly what I thought in front of him even though it might unleash terrible consequences. I did not doubt that my condition as an Aryan German offered me a level of protection from his racist, criminal mind, but no one would have reprimanded him had he shot me then and there.

"Someday you will understand what I'm doing for Germany and the world. We do not want to exterminate all races, only help each take its rightful place. After the war there will be a colony where all the Gypsies can live. I've heard Himmler, our *Reichsführer-SS*, speak on the matter himself. I can assure you he is a man of honor who always keeps his word."

I made no answer but merely bowed my head by way of excusing myself, and he walked me to the door. Night had already fallen. I did not want to turn and bid farewell again. That afternoon I had lost my final hopes of finding anything human in Mengele. He had completed his maleficent transformation in the six months he had been at Birkenau, approximately the same amount of time our family had been here. From war hero and loyal Nazi, he had become a bloodthirsty doctor with no regard for his patients, selecting people for murder with impunity.

Back at our barrack, I found that Ludwika had already put the children to bed. It was a relief to me not to oversee the routine that night. I was exhausted, drained of all strength. Discouragement had lodged itself immovably in my heart and body.

"So how did it go?" Ludwika asked tentatively.

"All right, in a way. He has committed to providing food for the children's school." My voice was flat.

"Well, that's good news."

"I'm not so sure. I sensed something sinister in that place. We have to be ready for the worst. Our fate is tied to the events going on outside these fences. If the Nazis lose, they'll want to erase all traces of their crimes. If they win, it'll be no skin off their backs to do away with us then. Only a miracle can save us from a slow, sure death."

Ludwika slumped under the weight of my somber thoughts. We were relatively young, and we wanted to believe life would go on, that we would find a way forward, but we were no better or different than the millions of people who had already died in Europe and half the world over in this war. Death did not pause to distinguish between the guilty and the innocent. It thrived on the hundreds of thousands of souls that joined its gruesome list of desolation each year. All of our names appeared on that list. Only a miracle could save us.

FOURTEEN

DECEMBER 1943
AUSCHWITZ

The end of the year was approaching, which would normally be a time of celebration and joy. But it filled us with uncertainty. Would we survive to see 1944? News had arrived of relentless bombings over Berlin and other German cities. The repercussions in Auschwitz were that the guards seemed preoccupied, drank more, and were always in their foulest moods. Many of them had lost family members, and some were starting to fear that their crimes would not remain unpunished forever. It was better to avoid them completely and go unnoticed.

Mengele stuck to his word. Things got better in the nursery school during October and November, but supplies started to dwindle again in December. The official explanation was that Allied attacks were making the transportation of material goods difficult, but, paradoxically, trains packed with Jews and other Nazi hostages kept arriving unhindered to Birkenau. Nazi logic never coincided with that of the rest of humanity. Hatred was an energy source for them that slipped right past us.

The Gypsy camp population was now decreasing month by month. Winter at the end of 1943 was also particularly brutal. Most barracks had neither firewood nor coal to burn. The nursery, the school, and the hospital were the only barracks allowed such luxuries.

The children could stay put, warm and clean, all morning, but in the afternoon, and especially the harsh nights, they had to be in the mud-caked, frigid barracks.

At the end of November I petitioned the commandant to allow the youngest children to sleep in the nursery and school barracks, but the request was denied. As the days dragged by, more and more children died, grew ill, or suffered the terrible symptoms of noma.

Camp morale was low, to put it mildly. So I was surprised when they sent us an Estonian Jew named Vera Luke to join the roster of teachers. The young woman had been a nurse in her country, and though she had a sickly, wan aspect, she was a breath of fresh air for the nursery school as we slogged through very dark days.

I gathered the team of teachers first thing in the morning before the children were to arrive, and we talked through the last few weeks. I was chiefly concerned with how we were going to face the winter in these starkly adverse conditions.

"I'm pleased to introduce a new colleague, Vera Luke," I said to everyone.

They tried to welcome her warmly, but most of my coworkers were also suffering the effects of the cold, malnutrition, and anguish over the desperate situation of the children.

Vera smiled and said, "When they told me I'd be working in a nursery school in Auschwitz, I thought they were mocking me, but now I see it's possible to create an oasis in a desert."

Smiling was an extravagance the rest of us had not allowed ourselves in many weeks.

"Thank you, Vera. Now let's see what supplies we're missing."

I started rattling off a long list that seemed to grow even longer by the day. When I finished, I glanced at the others. Their heads were hung low in discouragement.

"I think you're looking at what you don't have and what's standing between you and having nothing left at all," Vera said. "I've been in this hellhole for two months, and I've learned not to expect anything, to try to enjoy each day, and to not think about tomorrow. I suggest an act of rebellion. Let's celebrate Christmas!"

We all looked at her in alarm. For most of us, Christmas meant celebration and hope, but neither of those existed in Auschwitz.

"You all know I'm a Jew, but if we celebrate Christmas we'll give these children back a little bit of their faith. They'll have new hopes, dreams, aspirations. Please, don't let the Nazis steal those things from them too."

Vera looked at us with a radiant smile, her brilliant white teeth sparkling like diamonds before our weary eyes. I tried to envision my five children celebrating Christmas there. It was their favorite time of the year, but then the doubts started rolling in. How would we ever scrounge together what we would need? What could we offer them?

"But we don't have anything to be able to celebrate Christmas," I said, shaken. It was the first time since I had been leading the nursery school that I had not allowed myself to get excited about something for the children.

"We can work up a tree, decorations, and presents, even if they're really simple. We'll try to get a bit of sugar and flour to make cookies. The rest will just be carols and a little pageant," Vera said brightly.

The enthusiasm began to spread, and everyone started

talking at once. It became quite a clamor, and I looked at Vera. I understood what she was trying to do. She wanted us to be able to dream again, but I was afraid that a new failure would end up unraveling the shred of hope still holding us together.

"Very well, we'll celebrate the holiday. We'll try to get the guards to help us, though surely they'll oppose it. Lately they've been nothing but taciturn and bitter. We've only got two days to pull it off. We'd best get to work!" I said, talking myself into it as I spoke.

We spent the next hour planning and dividing up the work. Everything else on the day's agenda got pushed aside. The lack of food and our uncertain future were currently unimportant. Vera had reminded us that the best food for the soul was hope.

When it was time for the children to start arriving, I oriented Vera on her new tasks and, as we did every day, the teachers stood at the barrack entrance to welcome the pupils. We looked at the wide street covered in snow. The temperature had dropped so low during the night that most of the white blanket had frozen solid. The cold whipped our faces and easily trespassed our clothing to sting our skin. After ten minutes of waiting outside, we decided to go back into the building.

I motioned for my colleagues to sit at a table, and I

looked out the window. There was not a soul to be seen throughout the camp.

"Does anyone know what's going on? Why aren't the children coming this morning?" I asked nervously.

Zelma raised her hand timidly, and the other Gypsy mothers looked at her gravely. "The mothers are worried, and they prefer not to send their children."

"Why didn't you tell me this? What's going on? This is the only place in the whole camp where the children can be warm for a few hours and have a bit of decent food."

They could hear the bad mood in my voice. I felt betrayed by some of the women on my own team.

"They're afraid they won't see their children again if they bring them to school. Dr. Mengele has taken many of the twins and some of the Gypsy children who have eyes that are different colors. They don't trust us anymore. I've begged them to talk to you, but they say you're a German, a Nazi collaborator."

The final words were barely audible. Zelma clearly felt terrible to be the bearer of this bad news.

"That's ridiculous. Most of the children would be dead by now if it weren't for the nursery and school. Winter is a real problem. So many have died of starvation and the cold, but it's not our fault we can't provide more for them." I was angry.

One of the Gypsy mothers got to her feet and pointed at me. She started shouting all the things she had apparently been holding back for months, everything she thought I was doing wrong. "Your children get better food than the rest. They get to live in this warm, comfortable place. Most of us have lost at least one or two children, but you've kept all five safe and healthy. You're the doctor's favorite, but the question is, what are you giving him in return? Has he promised to protect your children?"

Her face was twisted with a terrifying hatred. I had always tried to do everything possible to improve the living conditions for all the children. I decided it was better not to answer. Instead, I stood and went to the door.

"Where are you going, Frau Hannemann?" Zelma asked.

"I'm going to go barrack by barrack to talk with each and every mother," I said, buttoning up my coat and heading out to the freezing street.

Silently, they all followed after me. Their presence was moral support. We went to the first barrack, and I entered with determination. The children and their mothers were huddled in the middle of the building, away from the walls. There was hardly any difference between being inside and being outside, though the reek of sweat, urine, and rotting wood took me back to my first days in Birkenau. The difficulties I had faced since then flashed before my eyes one by one. It was nearly impossible to remain sane in a place like that. Those mothers were true heroes, but fear had completely paralyzed them.

"I'm so sorry for the distrust between us. Life here in the camp is so hard. The winter is ruthless, and I know rumors fly about all sorts of things. We only want to help. We're offering you the only thing we've got, which is our very lives. We don't like having privileges," I said. "I've begged the commandant to let the children sleep in the nursery barracks, but they've denied my requests. My fingers are raw from all the petitions I write. Sometimes I run out of paper to write them on. Herr Doktor has given us some help. It's true that he also takes children for his experiments, but he himself told me they're researching to find a cure for the gangrene that's affecting our Gypsy children."

I paused for a long moment and looked into the faces hardened by hunger and fear. They seemed like ghosts floating in a dark cemetery.

"But you have to trust us. Your children will receive a little more food than they would if they stayed in the barracks, and at least they can be warm for a few hours. I have no control whatsoever about the children they take to the camp hospital, but I will try to keep them as if they were my own children. I promise you."

I knew there was little to nothing I could do if the

guards took the twins or any other children, but at least I could attempt to stop the transfer and demand an explanation for why they were being taken. The mothers motioned to their children, and the little ones followed us out to the next barrack.

For the next three hours, we repeated the scene in every barrack in the Gypsy camp. It was exhausting, and by the time we were finished, we were freezing and spent, but at least 95 percent of the children had been allowed to follow us. Then I went to the hospital while the other teachers began their classes. It was already noon, and that was when I typically visited the sickest children. I had barely crossed the street when I witnessed something truly shocking.

The guard Maria Mandel was walking through the snow dragging a little wooden sled. Sitting on it was a Gypsy child about five years old, dressed in nice, expensive clothes. The child seemed to be enjoying the sleigh ride. Maria stopped right in front of me.

"Prisoner, I want you to take care of this child. His name is Bavol, and he is the son of the king of the Gypsies in Germany. His family is one of the noblest of all the Gypsies. His parents were chosen by Herr Doktor Robert Ritter to represent the German Roma. They say that they were even crowned in Berlin three years ago, and the archbishop officiated the coronation. It must have gone to his father's head, because he organized a Gypsy rebellion in the Lodz ghetto, which is why they brought most of them here. The orders were to execute the parents, but there were no orders about the child. You'd better take good care of him. He's worth more than the rest of all those brats combined."

I was in complete shock seeing that beastly woman pulling the little prince on the sled. I looked at the child. He had such wide, dark eyes. His appearance was impeccable. No stain was to be seen on his blue velvet clothes.

"When classes are over, will you come for him?" I asked nervously. One never knew how Maria Mandel was going to react.

"Yes, of course," she barked. "If I can't get there, one of the kapos will come for him. The child is under my direct supervision. No one touches him." Then she bent down, smiled at the child, and gave him a piece of chocolate. I had the distinct impression that the boy was like a pet to her, something to keep her entertained and give her affection. We cease to exist when there is no one in the world capable of loving us.

The guard started walking again toward the barracks at the front of the camp, and I looked at Bavol. I held out my hand to him, smiled, and asked if he'd like to come with me. The little prince said nothing but did return my smile.

We went up the stairs to the nursery and I introduced him to one of the teachers. I studied the walls for a few seconds. The paint was dull in comparison to opening day, but it was still a wonderland in which to forget the tragedies of camp life.

"Do you like to paint?" I asked the child.

He nodded vigorously and dropped his arrogant posture to give me a big smile. I presumed that for years the world had treated the child and his parents like royalty, and now he was just one more victim of the cruel and arbitrary Nazi system.

The next two days were frenetic. Our team of teachers arrived two hours before class to prepare the materials, and I burned a path between the barracks and the office making requests for all that we would need. Dr. Mengele agreed to give us extra food that day, and a kapo showed up with a fir tree for the party.

We spent all morning practicing Christmas carols and staging a pageant. We wanted everything to be just right.

On the evening of December 24, Christmas Eve itself, the party was ready. The littlest children would sing two or three songs, the older ones would put on the pageant of Jesus' birth, and then there would be food for the children and their parents. We doubted that any of the guards would show up. For them it was easier to keep seeing us as animals or objects and thus avoid any hesitation when it came time to punish or kill us.

The celebration started right on time. Candles and garland throughout the nursery barrack evoked a distinctly Christmas ambience. The beautiful fir tree with little candles and ribbons turned the room into a spacious, homey living room.

The parents came in silently and got settled. Most of the men remained standing while the mothers angled for the best positions to see their children. Blaz and Otis were in charge of seating people to avoid any problems. We had strung up a long sheet as a curtain. Vera came out onto the makeshift stage dressed in a sort of tunic and addressed the audience: "Dear parents, grandparents, and brothers and sisters, today we are going to celebrate all together one of the holidays most beloved by children and adults alike, Christmas. The children have put a lot of love into preparing this program, so I ask you—"

Vera suddenly went stock-still, as if she had seen a ghost. I turned and first felt the cold that was seeping in through the half-open door. Then Maria Mandel appeared. Her uniform, impeccable as always, was partially covered by a large gray cape. People drew away from her in fear. We all thought that she was there to interrupt the event or that she would start beating the guests, but she merely leaned against the back wall and stayed quiet.

Vera found her voice again. "First the children will sing 'O du Fröhliche,'" she announced.

There was timid applause, and my sons helped pull back the curtain. The children were dressed with little black bow ties and suspenders. Their bright white shirts shone in the candlelight. They looked at Maja, their teacher, and began to sing while Blaz accompanied them on violin.

The beautiful voices of the youngest children fluttered between the walls of the nursery while snowflakes fell outside in the dark night. The chorus transported us all back to happier Christmases. Our minds sought out images of presents, anticipation, and the magic that wrapped the stable in Bethlehem that night. Melancholy started to spread throughout the room, eventually overtaking us all. Suddenly, one of the children began to cry, and it did not take long for all the children to join in as they recalled the happiness and gifts of Christmases past.

The tears drowned out their voices, first just as a whisper, then as a torrent that dragged us all down with the sadness. I looked at Adalia, standing with the little girls, and from afar beheld the beautiful pearls that danced in her blue eyes. I thought of Johann, of whom I had had no word since our fleeting visit in Kanada. It was our first time to spend Christmas apart since we were teenagers. Perhaps this would be our last Christmas. There would be no more special foods, no more singing in front of the fireplace, no more presents beneath the tree the next morning or children impatient to tear into the colorful paper, their eyes as wide as saucers and joy oozing from every pore of their bodies.

I tried to rise above it. We could not let the night be ruined by gloomy thoughts or sorrow over those who were no longer with us. I stood up beside the children, took Adalia by the hand, and began to sing. At first, my voice was alone in the crowded room, but then the other teachers joined in, and soon the entire room was singing the beautiful carol.

The little girls sang two more songs, and then the older children acted out Jesus' birth so gracefully. Emily was dressed as Mary, and Ernest was Joseph.

Then Zelma and Kasandra put on a puppet show for the children, who were sitting at their mothers' feet by that time. Bavol, the little Gypsy prince, sat at Maria Mandel's feet. She seemed to be enjoying the show, the first sign of actual humanity we had ever seen in her.

When it was over, everyone went to the tables and started eating. Though most of the adults had not tasted

any of those delicacies in far too long, they left nearly all of
it for the children.

Maria Mandel did not approach the table to eat. She
put Bavol's coat on him and slipped discreetly out of the
barrack. As she went, I wondered what kind of soul those
female guards had that allowed them to act with such brutality and cruelty. I also knew I would never get an answer.
Evil is much bigger than an antisocial behavior or a psy-
chological deficiency. Above all, it is a lack of love for one's
self and for others. The guard was acting like a mother that
night, but I did not know how far she would be willing to
go to save her new pet. Nazis always followed the rules. The
party was their life, and any infraction might cut them off
from the source of power and influence, turning them once
again into the nobodies they had been before. Hitler had
given them a reason to live. They were faithful dogs to a
heartless master, but at least the master let them taste the
leftovers of his cruel power.

An hour later, the families left the nursery barrack
with something like happiness. Within a few minutes they
would once again be in the insufferable reality of camp life,
but they all thanked us for the unexpected gift that held
out life to them, even for a moment. As the party drew to
a close, the teachers helped me clean up. When everything
was back in order, I put the children to bed. They were so

tired they hardly put up a fight. Blaz and Otis had each received a gift of a little slingshot, but they could not take them outside the barrack because they were forbidden in the camp. The twins had received a one-armed doll and an old, dingy horse, but Emily and Ernest thought they were the most precious toys in the world that night. Adalia was clinging to her new rag doll and gave me a kiss as she curled up in our bed.

I went back to the main room and began writing in my journal. It had been quite some time since I had written, perhaps in refusal to keep safeguarding my memories. I had hardly begun when I heard the door open. I hid the journal in my coat and looked anxiously at the shadow whose contours were forming in the doorway. To my surprise, it was Maria Mandel again. With her body slightly hunched, she entered and took a few steps toward me. I began to tremble. That woman was never the bearer of good news, and everyone feared her. She came closer, and in the candlelight I could see her eyes were red and her look was fierce.

"They took him," was all she said.

I knew she was talking about the child she had taken under her patronage, but I did not know exactly what she meant. I was too afraid to ask, though. She might react violently; maybe she came here to do something to my children.

"They took him. They just emptied the orphans' barrack. They took a dozen to the camp hospital, but the rest will cease to exist within a few minutes."

Her voice was hoarse, as if she had been crying for a very long time. I wondered, too, if she had been drinking, but she seemed sober that Christmas Eve night.

"Can I get you anything to drink?"

"No, I just didn't want to be alone tonight. Everything that's happened here . . ." She did not finish her phrase.

"I'm so sorry. He was a beautiful and intelligent child."

"What do you know about it, whore? You're a German woman with a bunch of trashy children by a Gypsy bastard. You're nothing like me. People like you are pure rubbish. Keep your compassion for yourself. Pretty soon you'll need it for your own brats."

She glared at me and, for a split second, behind the immense layers of pride and evil, I saw a dim flash of something human. Then she turned and marched out into the snowstorm. Her words had gone through me like fiery daggers. What had she meant? Was she threatening me or just trying to let out her rage?

All human beings are irreplaceable, of infinite value, and nothing can substitute the life that is taken. That night we were celebrating life, the birth of the Christ child, yet many more children would have to die, sacrificed to the flames of hatred and evil. I bowed my head and thought about the message of the manger: *Glory to God in the highest, and on earth peace, goodwill toward men.*

The war kept taking its toll of death and desolation that Christmas Eve. I tried to fill my heart with love. I did not want hatred to eat away my insides. I had to love even my enemies. It was the only way to keep from becoming a monster myself.

FIFTEEN

MARCH 1944
AUSCHWITZ

Winter was drawing to a close, but we knew that spring was still a ways off in Poland. Snow still partially covered the camp, and it would give way to ceaseless rain and mud and a sad death toll. Food remained too scarce. Some families with more influence in the camp hoarded what was meant for others. Women without husbands at the camp, people from smaller Gypsy communities, and children bore the brunt of the unfair distribution of the meager provisions. The most privileged members of the camp were my former German Gypsy friends. Several times I had gone to barrack 14 to appeal to them to change their ways, but the answer was always the same: they would see the children of other mothers starve to death before their own.

In a way, the growing laziness of the camp guards, who were more interested in staying drunk and forgetting about the war that was making its slow, inexorable way to Germany, made them inattentive to camp life. We heard tales of the dissolute life the female guards led with the SS soldiers. We even heard rumors that Irma Grese was pregnant.

The Germans had closed Antonin Strnad's school for older boys, and I was afraid they would shut down our nursery school at any moment. One Sunday morning, when we did not have class, my children were still sleeping in the back room when I heard a knock at the door. I got up and quietly opened the door, hoping not to wake them.

"Frau Hannemann, allow me to introduce myself," said a young woman with blue eyes. She spoke correct German, though her accent sounded Czech.

"Hello, please go ahead."

"My name is Dinah Gottliebova, and I'm a painter. Dr. Mengele has sent me to paint the portraits of some of the Gypsies at the camp. I wanted to request your help. Since you're the director of the school, you could perhaps help me gain access to the children and their mothers."

The young woman's request surprised me, but I knew Mengele to be keenly interested in anthropological and biological research. At first I could see no harm in painting the pictures of the schoolchildren. It would at least be something interesting for them, to shake up the torturous monotony of camp life. It seemed like just one more absurd Nazi command. The Nazis were obsessed with gathering information and keeping records of everything. Dinah was beautiful, with bright blue eyes and red-tinted hair. I later learned she was indeed Czech and that Mengele had asked her to document the Roma skin tones that photography was unable to capture.

"I can work up a list for you, and you could start tomorrow. I cannot guarantee that the adults will participate. People here at camp are extremely unhappy, and I'm afraid some would refuse."

"Thank you so much for your help."

"Would you like some tea?" I asked. The brew I was able to prepare was hardly recognizable as tea, but at least it was hot and tricked the stomach for a few minutes.

"Oh, tea is always welcome," she said, smiling.

It did not take long to fix our drink. When I came back to where she was sitting, she seemed lost in the murals on the walls.

"Who painted these?"

"Well, they're not as vibrant as they used to be. I did that one, but the bigger ones were done by a Gypsy named Zelma."

"They're very well done. Paintings like these saved my life," the young woman said.

"Really?" I was intrigued.

"Yes, just after I was brought to Auschwitz, someone in my barrack asked if I'd create a mural of Snow White and the seven dwarves, from the Disney movie. I thought the guards would punish me, but Dr. Mengele saw the mural and thought he could use my talents."

"Dr. Mengele is always looking for people who can further his experiments," I said, aggravated. I knew he was using all of us. He manipulated us like pawns to help himself go down in history with shining glory.

"It's true, but that's what saved me and my mother. We have better living conditions, plus I actually like what I do," she said, taking a sip of tea.

"It's been several days since I've seen Mengele," I commented.

"Surely he'll be at the soccer game."

Dinah had barely finished her sentence when we heard a woman shouting in the street. We ran outside and saw a mother about thirty feet away with her twin boys, Guido and Nino, who were four. Five days ago, an SS soldier had taken them despite my protesting. Since then, their mother came to the nursery constantly to ask about them. We ran to her. She was beating her chest, and her children were crying disconsolately. When we got closer we saw that the boys were covered with a torn blanket. They were shrieking uncontrollably, their dirty faces twisted in an expression of severe pain.

"What's going on with the children?" I asked, bending over to lift the woman from the ground.

"Good God! He's a monster!" she shrieked. Emotion made her speech nearly incomprehensible.

"Calm down, calm down. What have they done?" I asked, growing more scared.

"See for yourself. That fiend has mutilated them!"

I lifted the blanket carefully. Then I saw how the twins' backs and arms had been stitched together. The large wound was oozing pus and looked horrible, all discolored and swollen. Why in the world would anyone do this? The twins had literally been sewn together, their veins united.

Then I smelled it. The skin was rotting. Soon they would have a systemic infection, get gangrene, and die. I led them and their mother to the hospital. Dr. Senkteller and Ludwika were there. They ushered us in immediately, and while I left the mother with Dinah, the painter, I went to help my colleagues.

"Who did this to them?" the doctor asked, his eyes bulging in disbelief.

"Mengele." I practically spat out the name.

They looked at each other in shock. The deep, dirty wounds did not look like the work of a professional; they were more like the hacking and rough patching of a butcher.

"The infection has reached the bone. They might

survive a few days if we amputate the arms, but since we don't have morphine or antibiotics, the infection will spread throughout the body, and it will be a terribly painful death," the doctor said.

I was sweating, and nausea was rising up in me, but I forced it back down. Ludwika studied my face and said, "You look like you're about to be sick."

"I'm fine. What can we do for them?" I asked desperately. What was I going to tell the twins' mother?

A few months prior I had sworn to the camp's mothers that I would protect their children, but four pairs of Mengele's twins and another five Gypsy children had disappeared with the excuse of curing them of noma, though none of them had presented the slightest symptoms. But this was something else entirely. Mengele had gone completely mad. The only thing he cared about were his experiments.

"If we do nothing, the children will die in less than twenty-four hours. We can give them the little bit of morphine we've got left to put them to sleep, so they don't suffer," the doctor answered.

"Yes, thank you," I answered, unable to hold back two large tears that escaped from my eyes. I dried my face quickly and went out to the room where the mother was waiting.

She turned her imploring eyes on me, but when I shook

my head, she started screaming, crying, and beating her chest again.

"At least they won't be in pain anymore," I said, holding her tightly.

We stayed like that for a while, weeping in an embrace, until she calmed down a little. We left the hospital and walked slowly back to her barrack. Suddenly she threw my hand away from hers and tore off in the direction of the electric fence. I ran after her, but she had the advantage. From just a yard away from the fence, she leaped and grabbed on tight. A bright spark brought me up short. The woman convulsed momentarily until the charge threw her back. When I went up to her, I could see the terror on her face. Death had found her at last, but there was fear in the empty eyes that stared at the gray March sky.

I hugged her singed body while other prisoners began to gather. The kapos made me turn her loose and, after verifying she was dead, took her to the mound of cadavers that piled up every day behind the hospital barrack.

Dinah helped me stand up. Her serious face reflected the exhaustion that all that violence and death produced. Cruelty and evil were the clock hands that made Auschwitz tick.

We had hardly gone two steps when a wave of prisoners headed for the fence at the back of camp caught up with us. The soccer game was about to begin, and people crowded together to watch how the SS and the *Sonderkommandos* from the crematoriums competed on equal ground for ninety minutes. The prisoners loved it when an SS player fell down and went wild when the prisoners scored a goal against the Germans.

Looking one way, we could see the body of the twins' mother, still warm, resting on top of another dozen cadavers, but no one was paying attention anymore. Everyone was focused on the game, indifferent to their former comrade-in-arms. I looked toward the stairs leading to the sauna and saw Mengele. He was standing with one hand resting on the wooden banister. He was smiling in the direction of the soccer field, as if he were seated in a private box in a stadium. I was so furious I could not stop myself. I made my way through the crowd and walked straight to him. I went up the stairs, and he frowned in acknowledgment of my presence.

"Herr Doktor, two twins from my school have returned in a deplorable state. The doctors believe they will die within twenty-four hours." I willed myself to remain calm.

"Not now, please. I'm watching the game!" he said, trying to ignore me.

I stood right in front of him. I was just a bit taller than him and blocked his view. He brusquely pushed me aside, and I would have fallen in the snow had I not managed to grab on to the banister.

"What did you do to them, Herr Doktor?" I insisted.

He grabbed me with his cold, enraged hands and started shaking me.

"Cursed woman! I have been entirely acquiescent toward you. I have treated your family well, affording you great privileges. I pampered this camp with a nursery school and an orchestra, but I must continue with my research. Everything you've got comes from my institution. If it were up to the camp itself, all the Gypsies would have been gone weeks ago. Is that clear?"

I was stunned and terrified. In my heart I knew he was speaking the truth, but it was so repulsive I could not accept it. Right then everything in me wanted to die. I longed for the courage to throw myself against the fence like the twins' mother had done and end all the suffering.

"German children are going hungry and suffering the consequences of the war! Pregnant women are losing their babies! Old men and women are dying in the streets begging for bread! You cannot demand anything more from me; I am doing everything I can. If a few have to be sacrificed for the good of Germany, so be it. They end up saving many more. Do you want your children to be next?"

His red eyes looked like they were about to explode. He pulled out his Luger and held it to my head. I really thought it was all about to be over, but then everyone started shouting. The Germans had scored a goal. The doctor let go, put his gun away, and shoved me off the stairs. I fell hard into the cold, wet snow. I felt destroyed, completely depleted and about to give up for good. Then Blaz appeared and helped me to my feet.

"Let's go, Mom," he said, bearing my unsteady weight on his shoulders.

We left the crowd and walked toward the main road, then covered the short distance to the nursery barrack. It was still warm inside. I slouched at one of the tables, where our teacups from that morning still sat.

"I'll fix you some tea," Blaz said.

"No, I'll be fine. Go watch the game."

He went to our makeshift stove and heated up some water. In a few minutes, a steaming cup was before me. I felt the hot liquid descending my throat and thought of Johann. Surely he was watching the game from his side of the fence, so close and yet impossibly far away. I knew he would have protected me from that monster, but he would have lost his life in the process. Sometimes the things we lack or the obstacles we face become allies that help us endure. I decided then and there I would not be beaten. I would fight to the last breath. With the world falling to pieces around me, I would stand firm. Maybe spring would pull Auschwitz's starving inhabitants back from death's dark grasp.

SIXTEEN

MAY 1944
AUSCHWITZ

Rumors flew like sparks around Auschwitz. Sometimes the guards themselves or the kapos let slip an order or a sudden change in camp conditions; other times prisoners who worked for the Nazis as secretaries or in some other administrative position with access to privileged information spread the news. Somehow we always caught wind of what the camp authorities were planning.

The Allies had taken over nearly all of Italy, and people said that there would soon be another front on the Atlantic. The Russians were slowly pushing the Germans back toward their borders and ridding the Soviet Union of the Nazis. Allied bombing raids had destroyed the main German cities, and Hitler needed an ever-increasing supply of slave labor to keep making weapons. In April, the SS had taken away over eight hundred men and almost five hundred women from section BIIe. The Gypsy camp was steadily being emptied, as though we were the Birkenau rubbish pile being cleared out little by little. As our camp population dwindled to only those who were useless to the Nazis, living conditions grew even worse.

The only thing that seemed to improve in those days was the weather. The rain was constant, but at least it was not snow, and the temperature was bearable. Our work in the nursery and school had been drastically reduced. There were only about twenty children in each class, and the numbers dropped every month. I had not spoken with Dr. Mengele since my last encounter with him. I kept our communication to written reports about the work and requests for the children, which were systematically ignored. My assistants were showing signs of serious fatigue, and we faced the additional fear that they would be taken away as well.

In those days in May, one of the kapos, Wanda, brought us a little German girl named Else Baker. She was eight years old. Wanda was by no means the worst kapo in the camp, but nor was she necessarily an angel, which is why we were surprised when she said she had been caring for the newly arrived child for almost a month.

Else Baker was a beautiful little girl with fine features and an intelligent expression. She still looked soft and delicate—it was clear she had yet to face the hardships that most of the Gypsies in Birkenau had experienced. I went up to her and, smiling, said, "Would you like to stay here with us? You can be here from early morning until early afternoon."

She nodded, and as Wanda made her departure, I led Else to the school barrack. Though only seven, my twins, Emily and Ernest, were now there with the rest of the group. Lately we had begun accepting children of any age, though we had hardly anything to offer them beyond a few hours of distraction. The projector was broken, we had no more paper or school supplies, and, worst of all, we had no more food.

I had hardly opened the door when I met the desperate face of Vera Luke. She was rushing out and took no notice of the new girl.

"I was just coming to find you. They took the twins," she said in anguish.

I looked at her in disbelief. It was unusual for the guards to take children from the nursery school without informing us, but in Auschwitz nothing ever made sense. My chest started to close in, and I buckled forward. I had to do something. I tried to scream at my mind to get moving and go after them, but sheer panic was paralyzing me.

"We have to go to the secretary or look for the children directly in the sauna. If they're taken out of the Gypsy camp, they won't return," Vera said.

I let go of Else's hand and ran with Vera out to the road. There was no sign of them there. We thought they would have been taken to the sauna where Mengele often did experiments. We ran under a fine mist of rain and were soon drenched through. The grayness of the sky threw the intense green of the yards between the barracks into relief, and the forest swayed at the far end of camp. We ran up the stairs behind the sauna and stopped short at the door.

"Go back to the children," I told Vera. I did not want to get her in trouble. After all, it was my son and daughter who were at stake here. I was willing to risk everything to save them, but no one else should have to suffer the consequences.

I burst into the laboratory without knocking. Zosia was there with some files, just about to leave the room.

She looked up in alarm. "What are you doing here?" she hissed, looking frantically about.

"They've taken the twins," I choked out between sobs.

"It's complete madness today. The camp authorities have demanded nearly all the young men who remain, and another eighty women. It could be that your children got on the list by accident; they're just numbers to the SS," she explained.

"Maybe, but maybe not. They didn't let us know at the school. How are they going to make a mistake like that with *twins*?" I said in frantic disbelief. I could no longer believe a word she said. She had helped Mengele with his experiments.

"I don't know what else to tell you," she said, shaking her head. She waved to indicate that I should leave the office, but I managed to slip around her and run toward the laboratory.

I could hear Zosia's voice behind me as I threw the door open. Inside, the place had changed since the last time I had been there. It no longer looked like a research center. Now it was more like a torture dungeon where Mengele tormented innocent children. The walls were lined with different colored eyeballs in frames and horrid photographs of some of his experiments and containers of human organs of different ages and sizes. Some of the jars filled with disinfectant liquid contained deformed twin fetuses.

The doctor was at the back of the room with his back toward me, his pristine white coat partially blocking the bare legs of two children seated on the long cot. They must be my children. I ran toward Mengele, fully intent on attacking him if need be, but before I reached him, he turned and looked at me sternly.

"What are you doing here?" he growled.

I got behind him and saw the children. They were not mine. They looked up at me with sad little faces, begging me silently to get them out of there. Mengele dragged me by the sleeve out to the hallway.

"Have you gone completely mad? I nearly killed you once. You'd better not try your luck again."

"Where are my children?" I demanded. "Someone took my twins."

"They're not here. It must have been a mistake. I sign orders every day for the coming and going of prisoners. The factories need manpower, and some of the youth are leaving to work in other camps, but not the children," Mengele said seriously. Yet I sensed he was not telling the whole truth.

Then I heard the sound of trucks and ran to the door. The vehicles were parked in the road, and nearly a hundred soldiers jumped out and began rounding up Gypsies of all ages. I had no idea what to do. I should go back and protect the rest of my children from whatever the soldiers intended to do, but I should also go out in search of the twins.

Finally, I decided to look for my missing children. I knew that my assistants would give their own lives to protect the rest of the children in the school and nursery. I ran to the trucks. At first the prisoners put up no resistance, but suddenly an older boy threw a rock at one of the soldiers, hitting him square in the face. The young soldier began bleeding through the nose and shot the boy at once. The Gypsies around the scene jumped on the soldier and started beating him. It did not take long for the rest of the prisoners to follow suit. Men and women, the elderly and adolescents began throwing anything they could find at the soldiers and hitting at them with sticks and makeshift clubs. There were some gunshots, but the SS sergeant ordered the soldiers to fall back.

Some Gypsy adults helped the children and teenagers get up on the roofs, while others lighted torches and set the canvas coverings of some of the trucks on fire. The drivers reacted by speeding away toward the camp entrance, and chaos took over.

The soldiers drew back and holed up between barracks 6 and 4. The reaction of the prisoners had taken them completely by surprise. Typically there was little resistance to their brutality in Auschwitz, but that day they met their match.

I was proud of those Gypsies. Most people considered them antisocial, but they were the only ones who had been capable of defending their families and resisting being led to slaughter.

The soldiers shot and killed one of the boys who was throwing stones from a nearby rooftop, and I spotted Blaz not far away with his slingshot. A soldier was setting his sights on him. I ran and shoved the soldier hard, and the German lost his balance, sending the bullet harmlessly into space.

"Blaz, get off the roof and get back to our barrack!" I shouted. Then another soldier smashed the butt of his gun into my face.

Blaz dropped down from the roof and threw himself at the throat of the soldier. A group of boys joined him, and the two soldiers ran off toward the rest of their comrades.

Blaz helped me stand up. I seized his shoulders and demanded, "Have you seen the twins?"

He shook his head, but one of his friends pointed to one of the few remaining trucks parked at the camp gates. The canvas covering was ripped, and we could see a group of at least thirty prisoners trying to escape. The twins were among them.

Even though I ordered Blaz and the other children to go back to the nursery barracks, they all followed me. I ran to the truck, which was trying to turn but was blocked by the rest of the convoy ahead of it. Some soldiers were shooing away those of us who were trying to reach the prisoners in the trucks, but most of the SS was retreating. When we got to the truck, it managed to turn and headed for the gate. The kapos formed a human wall so we could not get through, but the sheer force of the people knocked them down, and we ran toward the truck. I reached the side and could see my children. We were only about ten yards from the fence. The soldiers were lined up on the other side of the gate, ready to shoot anyone who tried to leave the camp. Then I shouted at the twins to jump. They looked at the eight-foot drop, but Ernest crawled up the wooden side and grabbed Emily's hand. They leaped for the muddy ground and rolled for several seconds before coming to a stop. The truck passed through the gate, and soldiers quickly sealed the exit. Most Gypsies had managed to escape. Only a dozen or so had remained on the trucks.

People started running like mad for the barracks, afraid the Nazis would open indiscriminate fire with their machine guns, but there were no more attacks.

That night, all the camp's children stayed with our group of teachers in the nursery and school barracks while the rest of the Gypsies prepared for a further attack on the camp. They emptied the first few barracks and raided the warehouse and kitchen. They erected a sort of barricade, and we spent the whole night on watch, waiting for an SS attack.

At ten o'clock that night, with all the children asleep, a tense calm reigned over the camp, and we did not know when it would break. The children were scattered over the floor throughout the barrack, and all the teachers were resting at the door. The wooden floor was freezing, and my bones ached. The twins had refused to leave me, and I had one on each side of me.

Zelma whispered to me, "So I guess this is the end."

I did not know how to answer. I was thinking the exact same thing. Every day more and more trains of Hungarian Jews arrived, and it seemed we had become a nuisance to the Nazis.

"For some, their hour came right when they got off the train. At least we've been able to do something beautiful before dying," I answered, though I was not at all convinced it had been worth it to draw out the agony of the children who had fallen into Mengele's clutches.

"It's been a pleasure to know you and a real honor to work with you."

"Zelma, don't think about things like that. The Nazis need young people to work their arms factories. Surely you and the other teachers will get out of here alive. I've had a full life. I'm sad for my children, but who knows what kind of world would await them after the war anyway. Maybe death is a mercy for us all."

I had not given up; I was ready to fight to the last breath. It seemed to me that defending our lives was the last act of freedom that remained, yet death seemed so safe and secure that I was not opposed to the idea.

"Klaus, one of the boys, figured out that someone with a small frame can get out through the sauna latrines to the soccer field. From there they have to get by the crematoriums and then hide out in the forest," Zelma said gravely.

"That's madness. There's no way anyone would get that far," I answered.

"But some have over the past few months. Most don't get very far, but some have gotten away."

"We're surrounded by soldiers. It would be suicide to let the children go out through the latrines," I said, shutting the subject down.

She was quiet, and silence once again reigned. Auschwitz had become one gigantic crematorium, and we were souls in purgatory as yet uncertain of our final destiny.

I spent the rest of the night in an uncomfortable, light sleep. I listened to the breathing of the children who had managed to survive one more day in the camp. Then a sharp whistle awoke us at the first light of dawn, and we all went to the barrack doors to hear more clearly the voice that called over a megaphone from the front of the camp. People were standing in front of the buildings like groups of curious neighbors wondering what the ruckus was about.

I recognized the voice of Johann Schwarzhuber, the Gypsy camp's *Obersturmführer*. We had not seen him inside the camp much, but his shrill voice was unmistakable.

"Roma friends, it is not our intention, as has been mistakenly reported in the camp, to eliminate the Gypsies from Auschwitz. You are our invited guests, and after the war you will be able to live in a good place. Yesterday some of the men and women were being transferred to other work camps to help Germany in its war against communism. So that the tzigane population sees our goodwill, no one will be punished for yesterday's acts of rebellion. In the coming days, we will inform the elders of the community of the names of the prisoners we will transfer, with details about which camps they will be working in. Today the kapos will hand out a double ration of food, and tomorrow camp life will return to normal."

We looked around at each other in surprise. We did not trust the SS officer's words, but at least it seemed like the Nazis were calling a truce with us. Perhaps they feared the rebellion would spread to other parts of the camp. Two hours later, the kapos handed out food, and things did go back to normal.

Ten days later, the Nazis were true to their word and took more than five hundred prisoners. By the end of May, there were fewer than four thousand survivors from the over twenty thousand who had lived at the camp at that point last year, in May 1943.

As soon as the last group of prisoners left, conditions

in the Gypsy camp grew even worse. Trains were arriving to the platform day and night. Thousands of people were being marched to the crematoriums and disappeared forever as that dark spring drew to a close. For once in history, death's cold grasp snuffed out the life that the coming summer promised.

SEVENTEEN

AUGUST 1944
AUSCHWITZ

The unbearable heat seemed to anticipate the inferno we were about to experience. Our already scant water supply had dwindled to intolerable levels, food had been reduced to the point that many prisoners moved about the camp like automatons, and the death rate among children was overwhelming. Near the end of May, the Nazis had transferred most of my assistants. The two nurses Maja and Kasandra were no longer with us, nor were two of the original Gypsy mother helpers. The only ones left were Zelma and Vera Luke, who had become my right-hand woman. Yet we had fewer and fewer children to care for. The school barrack had been closed, as had some of the hospital barracks. Ludwika was the only health-care attendant left on-site.

The nights were stifling. But the heat and humidity were not the worst part. The most intolerable aspect of our unlivable conditions was the choking smell of smoke from the crematoriums and bonfires that burned incessantly that summer. The whistles of trains that arrived day and night from Hungary were nonstop. Sometimes two or three trains were backed up, and the prisoners had to wait inside for more than a day before walking to the slaughterhouses the Nazis had prepared for them.

We did hear some good news arriving from the front: the Allies were retaking France, and the Russians were continuing to march through Poland. The bombings were so intense that we saw bomber planes flying overhead day and night. Yet those of us holding on to life in the Gypsy camp sensed that the good news would not free us from the clutches of our captors.

Mengele was hardly ever at the Gypsy camp anymore. I only saw him when he was on the platform doing selections of the poor Hungarian Jews who came to Birkenau in ceaseless waves. From that distance, he seemed calm and composed, dressed with the same spotless precision as always, as if the upending of the Third Reich and the rapid decomposition of Auschwitz were of no concern to him. He did occasionally send us food covertly. In some way, he continued protecting my family. It may have been the last shred of humanity left to the man. The guards, on the other hand, were simultaneously dejected and furious. They killed prisoners at whim. They spent most of the day drinking, drunk as well on blood and hatred, like caged, rabid dogs lashing out as much as possible before being carted away.

Chaos reigned everywhere. The Nazis were overwhelmed at every hand, and we knew our camp was a headache, in a way, to Birkenau's authorities. A few weeks before, SS soldiers had liquidated the one Jewish family camp in Auschwitz. Over the course of a couple of days, nearly all the camp's inhabitants had been carted to the gas chambers in trucks. The Czechs had put up little resistance, though they were a much more numerous group than we were. In our camp, there were precious few young men left. Mostly we were children, women, and elderly. We were now easy targets for the Nazis.

That morning, the kapos and guards, who had hardly dared enter the camp in the last few weeks, did roll call and told us that one thousand prisoners would be transferred the next day to other camps. As we listened to the monotonous droning on of names, we were surprised to hear Else Baker's name. The child had spent part of her time with us since the spring.

I went up to her, took her hand, and congratulated her.

"Else, tomorrow you'll get to leave Auschwitz. I hope you'll see your parents soon," I said, stroking her hair.

"Thank you, Frau Hannemann," she said, smiling. She looked so happy. After a few months in Auschwitz, getting to leave that brutal purgatory, even if it meant going to a different one, sounded like the best news in the world. Then Elisabeth Guttenberger, the camp secretary, came up to me discreetly. She asked if I could walk with her for a bit, and we headed to the nursery barrack. I was totally exhausted. Hunger was affecting everything I did. I was chronically tired, and apathy was my most constant emotion. The only thing that kept me going was my children and the camp's children.

"It's over."

"What do you mean?" I asked, puzzled.

She took my hands and looked at me gravely.

"I cannot tell you everything, but the Nazis need all of these barracks for Hungarian prisoners. Gypsies no longer matter."

"They'll transfer some. What are they going to do with the rest of us? There will only be maybe three thousand of us by tomorrow."

"Look around you. The only ones left are unfit for work. The hospital has been dismantled, and all prisoner camp workers have been ordered to be at the main gate this evening. Tomorrow there will be no kapo, guard, secretary, or cook in the Gypsy camp."

We were at the edge of the camp by then and turned around. I looked at the crude wooden barracks, which were actually stalls built for animals. I studied the dusty road and the electric fence that ran the length of the borders of this forced Gypsy nation. We had been in Birkenau just over a year. In all that time I had only ever left my prison once; in some way that sick patch of earth was our home. I did not know what evil the Nazis had in store for us or why they thought we were so dangerous. Most of the prisoners held at Auschwitz had never committed any crime.

"I don't think Mengele would just let us be killed. Even now he's caring for my family in a way. Though he's done inhumane, reprehensible things, I don't think he'll let a German woman and her five children be killed."

I tried to act confident, but I knew that camp logic had no rhyme or reason. The most absurd orders were carried out with astonishing efficiency, though under any light they were clearly barbaric.

"Well, anyhow, I've sent a petition in your name to the commandant, requesting a transfer. I hope the answer arrives first thing tomorrow morning. I have everything prepared for you. We won't leave you and your family here," Elisabeth said, giving me a hug.

It felt like we were saying good-bye on a train platform, but we were not two old friends who had spent a lovely vacation together and now had to bid each other farewell; rather we were two castaways lost in the middle of the raging sea of war and human insanity. Hitler had declared total war. The Nazis had to do away with everything that did not aid or assist the march to final victory, and we were part of the war castoffs.

The afternoon dragged by in the camp. I gathered my children to eat something before we went to bed. I tried to keep a routine and structure each day to help them not be so anxious. The three youngest fell asleep quickly, and Otis soon followed. But Blaz was especially on edge that night.

"Tomorrow, most people are going to be leaving. Only a few of us will be left. People are saying they're going to do the same thing to us as with the Czechs. The camp workers aren't sleeping here tonight, and tomorrow they'll come by just to pick up the people who were on the list."

"I know, sweetie. Don't worry. Elisabeth is fixing things so that we'll be in the next transfer."

"There won't be any more transfers, Mom. We need to try to slip among the people who are leaving for other camps," Blaz said, as if it were easy for a family of five children to disappear before Nazi eyes.

"That's not as easy as you're making it sound."

"Maybe Elisabeth could get us put on the list."

"They've chosen the strongest ones and those who were distinguished in fighting in the Great War," I answered.

Blaz looked bitterly at the ground but soon resumed his argument. "We could get out through the latrines . . ."

"Your siblings are too little, and I'm too big," I answered.

"Well, we can't just sit here and do nothing." He folded his arms across his chest.

"We'll think of something tomorrow. Elisabeth might be able to get us out of here," I said, stroking his hair.

When the even breathing of my oldest son assured me he was sound asleep, I went out to the main room. I tidied everything up as best I could. There would be no classes tomorrow, and I did not know if there ever would be again, but I wanted to leave things neat and orderly. I lingered to look at the pictures on the walls, the little tables, the remaining shards of colored pencils. I was pleased. I remembered Ludwika's words from a few months before. All this work had not been in vain. In some way it had restored our sense of human dignity and our right to be treated as more than beasts.

I wrote my final reflections in my journal. I poured out my feelings more intensely than any other night of writing.

It's all coming to a close like a Shakespearean drama. Tragedy is inevitable, as if the author of this macabre theatrical work wanted to leave the audience with their jaws on the floor. The minutes are marching inexorably toward the final act. When the curtain falls again, Auschwitz will keep writing its story of terror and evil, but we will have become souls in purgatory haunting the walls of Hamlet's castle, though unable to actually warn anybody about the crimes committed against the Gypsy people. I miss Johann. I have no clue what has happened to him, but in the chaos overtaking Auschwitz, I fear that the Nazis will do away with every inconvenient witness to their crimes.

Soon I returned to bed, though not to sleep. Memories from an entire lifetime played out before me, one after another. I was happy I had married my husband. Some thought he was despicable because he was a Gypsy; to me, he was one of the world's greatest treasures. I thought of my parents. They were old, and I doubted they would have survived the war. They had also had a full, happy life. My children were beside me, resting as the intense summer sun began to peek over the horizon. I felt deeply afraid. I prayed for God to chase away from my mind all the bad omens. I accepted his will, and with this assurance I fell asleep just as the day dawned.

It seemed that our bodies were trying to relax that morning. When I finally woke, it was almost ten o'clock. I had nothing to give the children, but I heated up some tea. We sipped it silently while listening to the noises of the people lining up for the selection.

Someone knocked at the door, and I went to open it. Zelma stood there with her children. She had her few belongings wrapped up in a semblance of a sheet and strung over her shoulder. Her face was sad, but she gave me the gift of one of her beautiful smiles.

"Frau Hannemann, I've come to say good-bye. It's been an honor to know you."

"And for me to know you," I said, hugging her.

"I'll never forget your family."

The children tumbled out to say good-bye, and she hugged and kissed each, one by one, as we did the same to her son and daughter. When she was finished, tears were welling up in her big green eyes. I felt so sad as I watched them walk toward the Gypsies lining up.

Ludwika came out of the defunct hospital barrack and made her way to where we were. She was much less expressive than Zelma, but she said good-bye in her own way.

"Elisabeth told me she's getting an order for you all to be transferred to another camp. They never should have brought you here," she said, fighting back tears.

"Why not? I'm no better than anyone else here. Blonde hair, blue eyes, German parents—it's all chance. I feel like one of the Gypsies. I wish they would accept me as one of their own. They've lived so long like this, persecuted and despised by all, but there's a greatness in their hearts, a nobility the world has lost."

Ludwika wept against my shoulder. To the very end I was consoling those who wanted to help me in this impossible situation. As the children got distracted playing awhile, she and I recalled some of the things we had lived through together. It had not all been bad.

Then the Nazis ordered the prisoners who had been selected to get into the trucks that were parked between the kitchen and the warehouse barracks.

Most prisoners who were left went back inside their barracks before nightfall. The heat was stifling, but it somehow felt safer to be inside the wooden stalls. Yet I preferred to stay outside a bit longer, just looking and watching on that August day.

Around five o'clock Elisabeth came up to our barrack. She walked alone down the wide road of what felt like an empty, listless camp. As she approached, I remembered back to when the street was jam-packed with families trying to kill time by taking a walk before a meager supper.

The secretary stopped a few yards away from me. She

shook her head and did not come up the barrack stairs. She started crying and covered her mouth with her dark hand, trying to hold back the sob that ruptured the afternoon's calm.

"How long do we have left?" I asked serenely, as if the only thing that mattered at that moment was the schedule.

"They'll be here in two hours."

"Thank you. Thank you for everything," I said.

She turned and slowly walked back up the road. I went into the room and played with the children for the next two hours. We were waiting for the SS to burst in at any minute but, to my surprise, heaven granted us a little longer.

I wrote in my journal for a while and then left it on the table. I cleared my throat to tell the children what was about to happen, but then there was a knock at the door.

Dr. Mengele entered, dressed in a long black leather coat. He greeted us politely and asked if he could see me alone. I sent the children to our room at the back, and he and I sat at one of the tables as two old friends might do, yet this was not friendship.

He was quiet for a long moment and then put a piece of paper on the table.

"What is this document?" I asked, curious.

"It's a letter of safe passage. You yourself are not a prisoner of the Third Reich. With this letter, you can return to your home," he said seriously, his face darkened.

MARIO ESCOBAR

"We can go home?" I asked. I was more confused than happy.

"No, you yourself may go home. Your children must stay." He stated the facts tersely.

"My family is here. I can't leave without them. I'm a mother, Herr Doktor. You all wage your wars for grand ideals, you defend your fanatical beliefs about liberty, country, and race, but mothers have only one homeland, one ideal, one race: our family. I will go with my children wherever fate takes them."

Mengele stood and nervously smoothed down his hair. My words had unsettled him somehow. I was not the model of the Aryan woman he had in his mind.

"They will all be killed tonight in the gas chambers. They'll become part of a mangled mass of bodies; their corpses will be devoured by the flames and turned into ash. But you can go on with your life. You'll have other children and be able to give them what you couldn't give these. You've thrown your life away. Look at yourself; you're a ghost of who you were. You're nothing but skin and bones."

I smiled. At that moment I realized I had always been superior to him and all the assassins who ruled that inferno. They were capable of snuffing out the lives of tens of thousands of people within seconds, but they could not create

258

life. One good mother was worth more than the entire murderous machine of the Nazi regime.

I took my hand off the paper. For a moment I thought about throwing myself at his feet to beg for the lives of my children, but I stayed quiet with an inexplicable internal peace. Mengele retrieved the paper from the table and tucked it into his jacket pocket, and something that was no longer disdain yet not quite respect flashed in his eyes.

"Frau Hannemann, I do not understand what you are doing. This act of individualism is deplorable. You are putting personal sentiment above the good of your people. The National Socialist Party has attempted to do exactly the opposite. We are a national body in which the individual himself is unimportant. I hope you are sure of your decision. There is no going back."

The officer turned to leave. The children crept out once they heard I was alone again. They all hugged me at once. We were one united mass with six hearts beating in unison.

"They're going to take us somewhere better," I told them with a knot in my throat. Perhaps it was a lie, but I did actually believe my words.

The thought of death that day sounded sweetly of eternity. Within a few hours, we would be free forever.

The little ones soon went back to their games, but Blaz stayed beside me.

"Honey, I think you should make a run for it. We've got maybe fifteen minutes left. I've packed you the food I was saving for an emergency, and a bit of money. Don't ask me how I got it. I've heard people say that outside the camp, the Polish resistance helps prisoners who manage to escape."

"But I can't leave you," Blaz said, bewildered.

"Go give your brothers and sisters a kiss. They'll live through you. Your eyes will be their eyes, your hands their hands. Our family won't be wiped off the face of the earth completely."

Blaz started to cry. He hugged me, and I soaked in the warmth of his body for the last time. He said good-bye to his siblings, who hugged him indifferently and returned to their games, unaware of what that hug meant. His eyes drank them in, memorizing their skinny faces. With its voracious appetite, time always devours the memories and faces of those we love. Memory fights to hold on to them through the strength of tears and the painful sigh of love.

I put his hat firmly on him and walked him to the door. I cinched his bundle and wiped his face with a handkerchief. Then I gave him one last kiss before he headed toward the sauna. When he disappeared between the barracks, I heard a siren. My stomach tightened, and I held my breath. There was an eerie silence all over the camp, then the sound of motors and barking dogs broke in. I went back inside our barrack. My children were still playing. I sat down with them and started cutting out papers as the world disappeared at our feet, shrouded in fire and ash. I remembered Johann's smiling face and wanted to believe he would survive the destruction, that one day he would find Blaz and together they would rebuild the ruined edifice of our existence.

In those final moments, I thought of the smell of real coffee in our apartment and the minutes before breakfast when everyone was asleep under the shadow of my wings. *"Blessed daily life, may nothing break you, nothing wound you, nothing deny your beauty and the sweet strokes you paint in our souls,"* I wrote in my journal before closing its covers for good.

EPILOGUE

I did not want to remember. It is true that the camaraderie of those years and the broken dreams of our ideals were always flashing up before me, but I wanted that past to stay in a hazy cloud that covered over everything.

I tossed the school notebook onto the seat beside me and closed my eyes, trying to steady my breathing. The reading had taken a toll on me, like hiking too quickly up a steep mountain. I had spent the entire transatlantic flight reading, and I was tired but also overwhelmed by the distinct memories of Helene Hannemann. Images assaulted my eyes like a raging, vindictive whip. I can still see her being led away by the soldiers that night, August 2, 1944. The Gypsy camp was a madhouse of shouting and pleas, but she remained calm, like she was simply taking her children out for an afternoon at the park. My men had to offer bread and sausages to the Gypsies to convince them we were taking them to another camp, but Helene simply took the food and, after helping her children climb into the trucks, told them to eat slowly the final morsels of their lives.

I did not want to get too close. I could not explain it, but her courage had an effect on me. It filled me with doubts, made me question my creed. I watched her from afar. She was in the back of the truck. When the vehicle started to move, Helene hugged the youngest ones to her. The other prisoners wailed and carried on, beating their breasts in terror of the gas chambers, but she started singing a lullaby. Her voice wrapped around those wretched creatures and rocked them calmly. By the time the truck reached the gates and turned toward the crematorium, the shouting had quieted down, and the wailing ceded to the profound silence of death.

I stayed with the soldiers to search the barracks. We routed out a few Gypsies trying to hide from their fate, but the voice of Helene Hannemann kept humming the old lullaby in my head. Her words fluttered up with the ashes of her existence when I left the Gypsy camp that night, never to return. So much courage, so much love in the midst of the most absolute darkness: it blinded me for a moment. But I understood then that the fate of men is a mystery in the mind of the gods, and we ourselves were gods, though our twilight was drawing to an end.

HISTORICAL
CLARIFICATIONS

The story of Helene Hannemann and her five children is completely true. Helene was a German woman married to a Gypsy man. In May 1943, she and her family were sent to Auschwitz and held in the Gypsy camp at Birkenau. After Dr. Josef Mengele's arrival to Auschwitz, Helene was chosen to open and direct the camp's *Kindergarten*, a children's nursery school. She was a nurse, and Mengele chose her because he thought a German would do a better job than anyone else. Helene had several female Gypsy helpers, two female Polish nurses, and a Czech nurse named Vera Luke.

The nursery and school were housed in two barracks, which were stocked with school materials, a film projector, and even a swing set. Mengele employed the nursery school as a holding pen for the children he would later use as guinea pigs for his experiments.

From the evening of August 2 until the morning of August 3, 1944, the Gypsy camp was exterminated. Despite Mengele's promises, Helene Hannemann and her five children were murdered in the gas chambers. She was given the option to leave alone, but she refused to abandon her children. In the novel, Blaz has a chance of surviving so that the reader is left with at least a speck of hope, but the reality is that all five children died that night.

I have changed the names of the children and of Helene's husband, but I have kept the true names of the majority of the real-life characters who lived and suffered in the Gypsy camp at Auschwitz.

Ludwika Wierzbicka, Helene's nurse friend, was a real prisoner who worked in the Gypsy hospital. The entire medical team mentioned in this book was real.

Elisabeth Guttenberger, the camp secretary, was a real person who managed to survive both the Gypsy massacre and World War II.

In the profiles of the female Nazi guards Irma Grese and Maria Mandel, I have attempted to stay as close to historical reality as possible. It was rumored that Irma Grese, a very beautiful and very cruel young woman, was Dr. Mengele's lover who miscarried a child of his while at the camp. Maria Mandel, one of the cruelest guards, took a liking to a Gypsy child, as narrated in this book, but had to hand him over to die. Both Grese and Mandel were executed by hanging after being found guilty of war crimes.

Dinah Gottliebova (later, Dinah Babbitt) was also a real person. Mengele had the young Jewish Czech artist paint portraits of Gypsy prisoners.

The Gypsy camp nursery school at Auschwitz really did exist and was open from May 1943 through August 1944.

According to the official register, 20,943 ethnic Gypsies were imprisoned at Auschwitz, though many thousands more were murdered upon arrival to the camp, with no count or trace of their presence; and an estimated 371 Gypsy children were born at the camp. However, Auschwitz investigator Michael Zimmermann claims that there were really 22,600 prisoners at the camp, 3,300 of whom survived when they were transferred to other camps around the middle of 1944. The Gypsies came mainly from Germany, the protectorate of Bohemia and Moravia, and Poland, though there were some from other locations as well.

The two attempts to exterminate the camp were real events, as was the Gypsy resistance in May 1944, which delayed the camp's elimination until August of that year.

Himmler did not visit Auschwitz in the spring of 1943. The last time he was at the extermination camp was in the summer of 1942.

Josef Mengele was transferred to the Gross-Rosen concentration camp on January 17, 1945. He took with him two boxes of documents, while the rest of his research was destroyed by the SS before the imminent arrival of the Russians to the camp. Mengele escaped on February 18, slipping among the thousands of soldiers captured by the Allies. Under the false identity of Fritz Hollman, he escaped through Genoa to Argentina. Despite the high price placed on his head, Mengele was never captured, and he drowned, presumably while swimming, in Brazil on February 7, 1979.

In February 2010, a grandchild of a Holocaust victim purchased Mengele's diary. In 2011, thirty-one more volumes of his diaries were sold, acquired by an anonymous collector.

We do not know if Helene Hannemann wrote a diary, but we believe it would have been something like the first-person testimony of the protagonist telling her story in this book.

In 1956, Dr. Mengele traveled to Switzerland to see his son. It is believed to be the last time he set foot on European soil.

CHRONOLOGY OF THE GYPSY CAMP AT AUSCHWITZ

1942

December 16. Heinrich Himmler, Reich Leader of the SS, signs the decree to incarcerate the Gypsies in Nazi-occupied territory and to create a Gypsy camp at Auschwitz.

1943

February 1. The Gypsy camp at Auschwitz officially opens, though there were Gypsies already incarcerated for common crimes.

February 26. The first Gypsies arrive at the extermination camp.

March. Twenty-three transports with 11,339 ethnic Gypsies arrive.

March 23. Some 1,700 men, women, and children are exterminated after arriving at Auschwitz to control the spread of typhus.

April. Another 2,677 ethnic Gypsies arrive.

May. Dr. Josef Mengele arrives at Auschwitz as the medical attendant to the Gypsy camp.

May. Another 2,014 prisoners arrive to the Gypsy camp. The Gypsy camp nursery school is established.

May 25. Mengele orders the assassination of 507 men and 528 women to avoid a new typhus epidemic.

1944

April 15. Some 884 men and 437 women are transferred to Buchenwald and Ravensbrück.

May 16. The Gypsy camp prisoners resist their extermination so strongly that the attempt to eliminate them is halted.

May 23. Another 1,500 prisoners are transferred to other camps.

July 21. The last Gypsies arrive at the Gypsy camp.

August 2. Some 1,408 prisoners are sent to other camps. The rest, 1,897 men, women, and children, are murdered in the Birkenau gas chamber.

November 9. A hundred new Gypsy prisoners are transferred to the concentration camp in Natzweiler for typhus-related experiments.

1945

January 27. The Soviets liberate the remaining 7,600 prisoners held at Auschwitz.

1947

The first Auschwitz trial, in Kraków, Poland. Around forty former SS officers and soldiers are condemned and some are hanged.

1963

The second Auschwitz trial, in Frankfurt. Twenty-two Nazis are tried and seventeen are condemned.

GLOSSARY

Arbeit macht frei: Work sets you free.

baxt: luck

Beng: devil

Blockführer: block supervisor

Gadje: non-Roma, non-Gypsy

Guten Morgen: Good morning.

Kindergarten: nursery, school, and childcare center

Knirps: little boy

Obersturmführer: senior assault leader

Sonderkommandos: groups of Jewish male prisoners who
    were forced to dispose of corpses from gas chambers or
    crematoriums

Zigeunerlager: name by which the Gypsy family camp was
    known

DISCUSSION
QUESTIONS

1. Helene faces many difficult decisions, beginning with the choice to accompany her family as they're being led away by the police. What, if any, different choices would you have made?

2. When she agrees to go with the police, do you think that Helene has any inkling of what lies before her and her family?

3. The conditions at Auschwitz were almost too terrible to comprehend. As you reflect upon the horrors experienced by the prisoners, discuss the ways in which the physical torments of the camp impacted the inmates' minds as well.

4. Why do you think Dr. Mengele wants to establish the nursery school? What is its purpose for him?

5. Why do you think Helene agrees to manage the kindergarten? What are her reservations, and are they valid?

6. Describe some of Helene's bravest moments. Would you have been able to muster the courage and strength to do some of the things she does?

7. Name a moment or a scene that is either heartbreaking or heartwarming. Why is that moment significant to you?

8. How does one maintain dignity in the face of inhumane oppression? What is the value of struggling against those forces, even when all seems lost?

9. In a place like Auschwitz, what is the value of hope?

10. What would you say is Helene's legacy? Was her battle worth fighting? Why or why not?

11. What does this story tell you about the power of love? The power of sacrifice?

12. The author based this novel upon a real woman who lived and died at Auschwitz. How does the truth of this story change the way you read and experience it?

ACKNOWLEDGMENTS

The memory of Helene Hannemann and her family will remain forever in the pages of this book but even more so in the minds and hearts of those who read it. When none of those mentioned below remain, still many will know the immense value of this great woman and mother.

I want to express my gratitude to the Museum of Auschwitz, which allowed us a guided tour to visit and discover both Auschwitz I and Auschwitz II-Birkenau.

My gratitude also goes to the following: to the written testimony of Miklós Nyiszli, assistant to Mengele. To the work of Sławomir Kapralski, Maria Martyniak, and Joanna Talewicz-Kwiatkowska about the Gypsies in Auschwitz, *Roma in Auschwitz* (Oświęcim: Auschwitz-Birkenau State Museum, 2011). To the testimony of the executioner and commandant at Auschwitz, Rudolf Höss, who wrote a disgraceful book to clear his conscience, which nonetheless provides us with valuable details. To Mengele's biographers, Gerald L. Posner and John Ware. To the testimony of the Gypsy survivor Otto Rosenberg. To the heartbreaking account of Dr. Olga Lengyel, and to the journalist Laurence Rees for his book *Auschwitz: The Nazis and the 'Final Solution'* (London: BBC Books, 2005).

To Miguel Palacios Carbonell, distinguished member of the Spanish Gypsy community, who told me the beautiful story of Helene Hannemann and her family.

To the president of HarperCollins Español, Larry Downs, who has eyes and ears in a blind and deaf world.

To the whole team at HarperCollins Español, Graciela, Roberto, Jake, Carlos, Alfonso, and Lluvia.

ABOUT THE AUTHOR

Photographer: Elisabeth Monje

Mario Escobar, with a licentiate's degree in history and an advanced studies diploma in modern history, has written numerous books and articles about the Inquisition, the Catholic Church, the age of the Protestant Reformation, and religious sects. Passionate about history and its mysteries, he has plumbed the depths of church history, the different sectarian groups that have struggled therein, and the discovery and colonization of the Americas.

@EscobarGolderos

www.marioescobar.es

ABOUT THE
TRANSLATOR

Photographer: Sally Chambers

Gretchen Abernathy worked full-time in the Spanish Christian publishing world for several years until her oldest son was born. Since then, she has worked as a freelance editor and translator. Her main focus includes translating/editing for the *Journal of Latin American Theology* and supporting the production of Bible products with the Nueva Versión Internacional. Chilean ecological poetry, the occasional thriller novel, and audio proofs spice up her work routines. She and her husband make their home in Nashville, Tennessee, with their two sons.